AT YOUR MERCY

Tales of Domination
A Mischief Collection of Erotica

mischief

This novel is entirely a work of fiction.
The names, characters and incidents portrayed in it are
the work of the author's imagination. Any resemblance to
actual persons, living or dead, events or localities is
entirely coincidental.

Mischief
An imprint of HarperCollins*Publishers*
77–85 Fulham Palace Road,
Hammersmith, London W6 8JB

www.mischiefbooks.com

A Paperback Original 2013

First published in Great Britain in ebook format by
HarperCollins*Publishers* 2012

A catalogue record for this book is
available from the British Library

ISBN-13: 9780007534876

Set in Sabon by FMG using Atomik ePublisher from Easypress

Find out more about HarperCollins and the environment at
www.harpercollins.co.uk/green

Contents

CONTENTS

Stranded
Rachel Kramer Bussel

I'm wearing my shortest skirt – white and flaring right out, like a tennis skirt – and no panties, along with a skimpy white tank top, through which my nipples are clearly visible, and platform wedges, as I sit on the barstool at our friend Colin's new restaurant, the latest of eight he owns. I'm only five foot three, but height isn't important from my perch. My almost black, sleekly styled straight hair falls just past my shoulders, long enough that I can swish it around or run my fingers through it. I'm wearing a little butterfly clip in my hair on one side, and stark, dramatic black eyeliner that makes my brown eyes pop, plus bright-red lipstick with shimmering gloss that makes me look even paler than I normally do, emphasising the dramatic colour.

At Your Mercy

Next to me is Jake, my lover, my boyfriend, my top – and my wardrobe coordinator. When we get dressed for an evening out on the town, he tells me what I should be wearing, from how to do my hair to whether to wear makeup to whether I should insert a butt plug in my ass. Sometimes I'm fresh-scrubbed, wearing a ponytail and an outfit more appropriate for jogging than for fine dining, what he calls my slutty cheerleader look, even though on the outside it's totally wholesome; he says the slutty part is something that those who know what to look for can just tell about a girl like me. Sometimes I'm in basic jeans and a sweater, incognito, in a way; he says that, when I'm dressed down like that, even those attuned to naughty girls don't have a clue, that it's our dirty little secret, to be revealed at his behest – or not. I have a walk-in closet full of four years of clothes he's purchased for me or that I've amassed, and, while fashion is a favourite pastime of mine, being Jake's plaything is my number-one hobby – or avocation, if you will.

He bought the tank, skirt and shoes for me; I'm more of a colour girl, when (occasionally) left to my own devices. I like to play up bold, striking colours that garner as much attention as the tattoo on my left shoulder of a purple dragon. Plus my breasts are big enough that I really should be wearing a bra, a fact he knows very well. When I don't, not only are they visible, they also bounce heavily against me with each step, reminding me

2

of their presence. 'I like being able to see those pretty nipples,' he told me while I was getting dressed, as he came over and plucked from my hands the T-shirt bra I'd been planning to wear. I know what he really meant was that he likes seeing other people noticing my nipples, ogling me quite obviously, sometimes accompanied by smirks or winks, allowing Jake to be a voyeur by proxy. Showing me off has always been something he's enjoyed, a bonus to our ongoing play, and under his tutelage I've become quite the exhibitionist. Sometimes he'll make me flash a car driving next to us on the highway, or he'll drop a credit card on the ground at an opportune moment, so I have to bend over and bare my bottom just when the car salesman or manager or waiter is standing there. If I ever refuse, the punishment will be far more embarrassing.

At first, I was a little concerned about this delight he took in my risqué attire; I loved the games we played, but wondered if Jake's lack of jealousy meant there was something wrong with him, or me, or us. Then I realised that it gave me a chance to show off and flirt and have fun in a safe way. I'd had lovers who acted like their mild jealousy was no big deal, only to later find out that even a smile at a stranger on my part could incite something in them I couldn't undo. With Jake, he'd made it clear that he wanted me, the core of me, the heart and soul of me, and if he had that – had my devotion – a few little harmless peeks and looks wouldn't matter. I was his to show off, but I was definitely his.

Technically, our relationship was open, but it came with boundaries and rules, and neither of us had fully taken advantage of that openness yet, save for some make-out sessions and heavy petting at parties in front of one another. The frisson of sexual energy passing between other people and back towards us was enough to recharge our erotic spark, to make us fully aware we were capable of choosing each other over and over again, even if other possibilities dangled in the air. 'That older man asked me if you'd suck his cock,' he told me after one of our early parties, as he shoved his fingers between my legs in our doorway. I'd shivered at the thought of them having such a conversation. 'I thought about telling him yes, then blindfolding you and making you suck his cock, thinking it was mine. Maybe another time. Tonight I want you for myself,' he'd said, before taking me roughly, tossing me on to the bed, pinning me down, both wrists in one hand, another twisting a nipple, while he slammed his cock into me in one deep, penetrating thrust.

The light bulb had finally clicked at another party when I'd watched, champagne in hand, as a sweet young thing I could've eaten for breakfast flirted up a storm with Jake, tossing her masses of blonde hair over her shoulder, gazing at him with utter adoration, letting her breasts not so subtly brush against his arm repeatedly.

There was something about seeing my Jake, in a suit, which is not really my thing but he wears them so well, chatting up this girl in a skimpy dress that probably cost a few hundred dollars while I wore artfully shredded jeans and a tight black lace top.

I admired him anew, and liked that he was being hunted down by other women, but would be coming home with me. He's extremely skilled in the art of flirting, and I smirked to myself as I watched him lean in towards her, heard her giggle but not whatever he whispered so close to her ear he may as well have kissed her. I got wet thinking about him doing to her some of the things he does to me. I got so lost in my fantasy of all that blonde hair swirling around her head as he held her in place while she sucked his cock, my fantasy vision so realistic that he startled me when he came back and whispered in my ear, 'Having fun?' I blushed, and asked him about the girl. My zest for the details made me see that Jake wasn't to be faulted for wanting other men to look at me; it was more like he was dangling me before their eyes, saying *look but don't touch* – except if I give you permission.

And of course men are going to look at me in the outfit Jake had selected, with my nipples practically right on the bar alongside my vodka cranberry. We shift to a table and, even though I'm not that hungry just yet, he encourages me to order whatever I want, and I select a glorious host of appetisers, from shrimp cocktail to grilled oysters to prosciutto-wrapped asparagus, along with a fruit and cheese plate. I wouldn't have to eat it all at once.

He takes my hand over the table, stroking it, his dwarfing mine. I love the way my hand fits into his, safe and secure and full of promise, whether we're just resting there, almost as if by accident, or squeezing tightly. This time, he runs his thumb along the pad of my palm, sending a shiver through my body. I catch a breeze in the air and my nipples stiffen, just as the waiter arrives with our oysters. 'Ma'am,' he says, and I try not to giggle. I'm not really the 'ma'am' type, by age or inclination, but I smile at him. It only takes a second or two for his eyes to rake over me, but I notice, and I am sure Jake notices, because his feet trap mine under the table and his hand squeezes me harder.

'Thank you,' I say, making room in front of me for the oysters, while he sets a plate of cheeseburger sliders before Jake. He is more the food snob than I am, and loves to test out the latest new hip foodie restaurant, even if their fare is nothing more than an overpriced attempt to cater to a crowd that wants to feel like they're getting their money's worth. We sip our drinks and the icy cool vodka cranberry works its way inside me, making me flush with that early buzz alongside my arousal. He watches me as he sips his wine, knowing exactly what even that little bit of alcohol will do to me.

We each order steaks, and then our array of appetisers arrives. We dig in, each of us lost in an almost orgasmic oral reverie at the exquisite tastes. We smile at each other, occasionally commenting on the tastes, but mostly saving our mouths for the mini feast. Jake traps my feet between his, pressing them together, letting me know he's aroused, and that he's still in control. I'm savouring a piece of shrimp when the awful sound of Jake's cell phone going off pierces the air. He looks at it, frowns, then picks up. I wait for a minute, then two, then give up and go back to eating.

'Honey, I've got to take this,' he says. 'I'm sorry. I'll make it up to you.' Jake doesn't look remorseful so much as determined, his mind already prepared to deal with whatever urgent work crisis has come up; it's a look I recognise well from our two years together, and one I know from experience brooks no argument. Work and I run a constant race for his attention, and work almost always wins, though only in true emergencies would he abandon me like this. We'd discussed this issue endless times and I'd grown grudgingly used to these occasional absences.

He's off with a quick kiss on the cheek before I can even fully process it, and I sit there facing a table full of food I'm not sure I want to eat now, with more on the way. 'Is everything OK, ma'am?' It's the same waiter, and I smile weakly.

'Great, thanks,' I get out, and pick up a piece of brie

and nibble on the edge. I can't help the moan of delight that escapes my lips, and catch an answering smile on his face. It is truly divine, and I devour the rest in two quick bites that leave my tongue in an ecstatic state, the echoes of the exquisite tastes lingering. I shift in my seat, suddenly hungrier than I've been all evening. Jake does, in fact, know how to pick 'em, and, while part of me wishes he could taste what he'd surely enjoy as well, I'm not going to complain about having to eat all the shrimp by myself.

It isn't until I've finished my last spoonful of the best s'mores I'd ever eaten, layers of dark chocolate pudding interspersed with graham cracker and topped by a triangle of toasted marshmallow that actually dripped off my spoon on to the table if I didn't bring it to my mouth in time, that I realise I don't have my wallet with me. I'd switched purses to an extremely small one holding only my lipstick and keys, because part of our arrangement is that, when Jake wants to eat at one of his fancy restaurants, he pays. 'Please don't take your phone, Jessie,' he'd urged – another ongoing battle is how much internet usage is acceptable at the dinner table – so I'd reluctantly left it at home.

So I'm stranded. My mouth is still twitching in delight as the last vestiges of the s'mores linger on my tongue, while dread starts to build in my stomach, the opposite of the butterflies I felt when Jake slipped his hand into the back of my panties, resting his fingers lightly against the crack of my ass as he led me to our table. Now I'm trying not to look frantic, to seem as serene and satisfied as anyone who's just enjoyed the hundred-dollar meal I've consumed. But the adrenalin coursing through my body won't let me simply lean back against the plush leather seat and feel satiated after what has to have been one of the most delectable meals of my life.

I scrape the spoon against the edges of the cup and think frantically of some way out of this, when I see Colin, the owner and head chef, coming my way. 'How was everything, Jessie?' he asks, that same slightly leering smile he uses every time I see him stuck to his face. I don't mind, because it's all in good fun, although an extra tremor runs through me.

'It was divine, truly. Look – I didn't leave a drop.' He leans over but manages to stare at my tits while he does, and, despite myself, they harden. 'The only thing is … I'm having a little problem. I don't have my wallet or any cash on me and Jake had to run out and I can't reach him, so could I run home and pay you back later tonight? It won't be long.'

Colin picks up my spoon and idly lets it dangle from his fingertips. 'You know, Jessie, I'd love to help you out, but this is a place of business, my place of business, and I can't let people just walk out without paying the check. That would be highly unprofessional of me. Maybe you can find a way to work off your … hundred and eight dollars, plus tip.'

I lick my lips, tasting the remnants of our meal and my sweet lipgloss. 'Sure,' I find myself saying. 'I'm great at dishwashing and know my way around a kitchen –'

Colin presses a finger to my lips. 'Stop right there, my dear. That wasn't what I meant, and I don't think it's what Jake would want you to do. He told me you don't like to get your hands dirty – but your mouth, that's another story.'

A huge wave of mortified, arousing heat rushes over me as I realise exactly what's just happened – Jake planned this. He asked me to wear this outfit specifically so I'd get stuck and 'owe' Colin a hefty bill. And from what I can gather from the words that have just left Colin's mouth, he wants me to pay for it with my body.

The thought makes me cold, then hot. Suddenly I'm not panicked and don't want to cry; I'm wet and hungry between my legs. I'm aching the way I ache when Jake tells me what a slut I am, how he wants to take me to a party, strip me and leave me there for anyone to have a go at. He likes to tell me that as he eases a fourth finger into my pussy, then orders me not to come just as I'm about to. This situation is as maddeningly delicious as that order. He wants to share me, in the most naughty way possible. He wants to whore me out to pay for my dinner. I wonder what Colin will want for the amount that I owe him?

He stands up then and drops the spoon on the table

so it clangs. I can see his erection pressing against his pants and this time, when I lick my lips, it's for an altogether different reason. If Jake had truly left me like this, I wouldn't have just been angry, but hurt and betrayed. We're not the types to let each other down or let work take priority. But we are the types to want to push the envelope, to force each other into new situations we'd never get to on our own, and this is certainly one of them. I decide to pretend I'm playing the role of the slutty woman who'll do anything to make up for her lack of payment – after all, I already look the part, and if Colin were to feed me more of that s'mores I'd probably let his entire staff gangbang me, it was *that* good.

But I'm not in the mood for food any more, even gourmet desserts. I follow him through the kitchen, the stares of the men and women chopping and sautéing making my nipples press harder against the thin tank top. I'm suddenly sure they can tell I'm not wearing panties. I brush against one woman who I'd thought was so intent on plating a mozzarella and tomato appetiser she hadn't noticed me, but the smile she gives me makes the air between us sizzle. It's a hungry smile, a predatory smile, a smile that says, *I want you when he's done*. No wonder the kitchen is so hot!

Then we're alone again, Colin tugging me away to stare directly at me, as if trying to figure me out. The more he looks at me like that, the more my mind starts to waver and wonder whether I really am in trouble, to wonder just how much of a setup this is. Could Colin truly have thought I would stiff him? I want to say something cute like, 'Do you do this with everyone who can't pay their check?' but the words stay in my mouth. 'Wow' is all I manage when Colin leads me back into his office, a cluttered but somehow still homey cube of a room cluttered with papers, open cookbooks, a laptop, a desk, chair and small couch.

'Was that "wow" because you didn't think I'd drag you back here, Jessie?' Colin's voice makes me tremble; it's low and rough and somehow menacing. 'I was watching you, you know. I was watching you eat, watching you enjoy the food I crafted with my own hands. I saw what it did to you. I saw these nipples –' with that he pinches them hard, so hard I almost cry out, but instead let the noise travel up through me, then silently back down, the pain bringing tears to my eyes '– and I knew how wet you had to be, how sad for Jake that he wouldn't get to taste them.'

He bends down and bites one nipple roughly through my tank top, so I barely have time to process the fact that I was right – the two of them have colluded to make this outrageous encounter happen. I wonder if he's told his staff, or if they're simply used to random women joining him in his office.

12

Colin is doing much more than tasting my nipples; he's lifted my tank top and, after licking my cleavage and sighing in contentment, gone back to the left one. He clamps his lips firmly around the bud and laps at it, the sucking sensations becoming stronger and stronger until I feel his teeth sinking into my flesh. I don't realise I've been holding my breath until it eases out of me and I race to get more air.

'I have something for you, Jessie,' he says, and, while I'm curious, I'm also disappointed that he's removed his mouth from my buds long enough to speak. 'Aren't you going to ask what it is?' he asks, grabbing my chin so I have to look at him.

He digs his fingers into my flesh, then drops them while I haltingly get out, 'What is it?'

The smile he gives me is pure wickedness, one that could've been copied from Jake, but with a different twist. Jake enjoys hurting me for his own mysterious reasons; the rush of energy he gets from breaking me down to my barest, basest level is something you can almost see puffing him up. Colin's look is different; I get the impression that he wants to know how turned on I am by all this. Now that we both know I'm more than happy to 'pay' for my meal with my body, he is free to push me to my limits.

While I'm staring back at him, he grabs my tank top and rips it down the front. 'That's much better, don't you think?' He swats at my tits with his hand, lightly at first, like a tennis player lobbing a ball across a court, more for the sound than the impact. When I stare right back at him, not flinching, not letting him see how my pussy reacts, he hits me harder, tilting his hand so he gets the side of my breasts, then directly against my already sore nubs. 'Hold these pretty breasts for me, Jessie,' he says, and my hands automatically shift to squeeze them, offering them up to him. Out of the corner of my eye I catch a glimpse of something metallic whizzing through the air before it strikes one nipple like a gong, then the other.

When I dare to glance down, I see that the outside of a long, skinny spoon is what is striking each nub, and I hold on tighter to my tits so he has an easier target. The spoon strikes me over and over, hammering into my nipples until the heat and pain merge into one glorious sensation. He pauses, then takes each nipple between his thumb and forefinger and twists hard, the spoon trapped between my breasts while he makes his point. He looks at me again, his eyes burrowing into mine, and I simply blink back until I can't pretend any more, until I have to let out a gasp, then bite my lip as his hold on my nipples deepens. 'I guess you're trying to tell me you can take even more, aren't you? Good thing I have these nipple clamps Jake gave me.'

This time I suck in air at the sound of Jake's name.

14

It's so dirty, so wrong, that Jake has given him so many pointers, that Jake is almost topping me by proxy, and yet all my energy is focused on Colin.

'Hold them again,' he says, and I do, presenting each breast for the tweezer clamps. Colin tightens them just a wee bit tighter than Jake usually does, and my breath comes out in rougher, louder blows.

'Take off your skirt, Jessie,' he grunts, and I drop my breasts, feeling the clamps shift and the weights on the ends tug on them as I do his bidding. My white skirt drops to the floor and I step out of it. 'I have something I bought for you, too,' he says, and takes another clamp out of his pocket, dangling it in front of my eyes. I know it's for my clit, and I'm tempted to smile. I've never had one there before, but I've thought about it, and certainly Jake's tortured my most sensitive spot more than enough times to let me know I can take a lot there too.

Colin's fingers slide along my wetness first, and he murmurs his approval. 'Very good, Jessie,' he says. 'I'd have been disappointed if you weren't nice and wet for me. You don't want to disappoint me after that meal, do you?' he asks before shoving three fingers deep inside me.

'No, I don't,' I say, trying to sink down to get more of his touch, but he pulls out and lifts me up with a hand on each hip. 'I'm gonna fill that pretty pussy, don't you worry.'

Then he's kneeling before me, first priming my clit with his lips, his tongue zooming in on its core, pressing hard against it, then sucking, until I think I might come. Just when I sense myself rushing towards that blissful reward, he pulls his lips back and fastens the clamp around my now extremely engorged clit. The pain is intense, and I'm standing with nothing to hold on to, nothing to lean against. I look around frantically and settle for clasping my hands behind my back, entwining them and willing myself not to tremble so much I fall.

'Now was there something you wanted, sweet Jessie?' he asks, standing again to press his hand against the back of my neck and draw me close enough that his chest meets my adorned one, his knee rubbing against my wetness.

'Your cock,' I whisper, already picturing how it will look, what it will feel like.

'I didn't hear you,' he says, pressing more firmly on my neck. 'Say it much, much louder for me. Say it so my staff out there can hear you.'

Oh God. He means that, which I soon find out when I say it in an outdoor voice, but one that's certainly not a scream. He twists my lower lip the way he did my nipple earlier. 'Do you want me to parade you around out there, Jessie, maybe make you go up to each and every person in that kitchen and tell them exactly what you want? They deserve to know, especially your waiter

16

tonight, who's not going to get a tip – unless I bring him back here.'

I do scream then. 'I want your cock!' I yell not so much because he's making me, as because what he's just said has made me painfully aware that I can't wait another minute. He takes my hand and brings it to the front of his jeans, and I hiss when I feel how hard he is.

'Take it out, Jessie,' he says, watching me fumble with his zipper and then peel down his black briefs to reveal an extremely large, long circumcised cock. I see the pre-come at the tip, and my insides tighten at the prospect of having him inside me. He kicks off his shoes, strips out of his shirt, jeans and boxers and lies down on the floor. 'Get on top of me, Jessie,' Colin orders me.

I'm on the floor straddling him in seconds, the clamps still working their magic. I take him inside me and for a moment it's not the frantic frenzied version of flirting and fucking we've been doing. I'm not the girl stranded without any means of escape in this man's kitchen office with his employees outside. I am simply a woman with a man's glorious cock filling me up while I stare into his eyes. Yes, I have nipple and clit clamps attached to my body. Yes, it's the first time, but in a way it doesn't feel like it; it feels like I've known his cock before, like his cock and my pussy belong together. He smiles at me and all hints of power and control melt from his eyes. He holds me gently, his hands on my hips, and I tilt forward, my breasts bouncing.

Then I smile as I squeeze him and lean down to lick his lush lower lip. I kiss my way along his neck and focus on squeezing him as tightly as I can until I have to just let go. His hand shifts so he is stroking the rim of my anus, the tender puckered ridge, and I lose it. All the built-up excitement and fear and arousal and denial catch up with me and I have to lift my hand to bite my finger so I don't scream again. The tears rush out of me unexpectedly; I didn't cry before, but now, when I am not afraid but totally blissful, they are there to caress me, rewarding me for a job well done.

'I'm almost there,' Colin grunts out, and soon he's pushing me off him, unclipping the clamps, and splashing my breasts with his come. I smile at him and bask in the warmth and the fact that he has so much of it for me. No sooner is he done than he's grabbing for his phone to take a photo. 'I promised Jake,' he says, and a blush creeps over my face, warming me in a whole new way. They didn't just talk about how I'd come to be in Colin's office getting fucked, but exactly what would happen in it. It's mortifying, but it makes me very, very wet, as I'm sure Jake knew it would.

Suddenly, Colin's phone rings. He answers and I hear Jake's voice: 'Hi, Colin, it's Jake. Is Jessie still there? I just realised I left her without any money.'

Colin smiles and passes me the phone, and I talk to my boyfriend, not caring that another man's come is dripping down my body.

'Honey, I'm coming back with my wallet to take care of the check. See you in ten.'

I hang up, pretty sure Jake's going to let me know when the jig is up. Or maybe he won't. Maybe Colin made that part of it up and Jake never intended me to fuck him. I'll find out. One thing I'm certain of: Jake will find a way to make sure I know my place: wherever he wants me to be.

Late
Elizabeth Coldwell

You've been expecting me for the last twenty minutes, and I'm still no closer to arriving. Tell a lie, the train's just started its slow, trundling progress along the stretch of track from Farringdon to Barbican. With nothing more in the way of hold-ups, I should be at the station within a couple of minutes. From there, it'll be a hasty dash to your apartment. But there's no way of covering up the fact I'm late.

I didn't deliberately set out to disobey you; I've never been one of those bratty bottoms, forever seeking ways to provoke my master and earn a harsher punishment. When you sent the message this afternoon telling me to be with you by six, no later, I made sure to be away from my desk by quarter-past five. That should have given me plenty of time to make the journey to your apartment; I just didn't count on a signal failure stranding me between stations.

Tense as I am, I can't help my mind drifting to thoughts of what you'll do when I finally arrive, stammering apologies and explaining why this delay really wasn't my fault. Your punishments are never less than inventive; half the time they don't even involve you laying a finger on me. I'll never forget the time I arrived at your apartment with a bottle of Liebfraumilch, because the corner off-licence didn't have the Riesling you'd asked me to bring. How was I to know you can't abide the taste of sweet white wine? That evening, you made me walk the seventeen floors to your apartment, rather than taking the lift. By the time I reached you, my lungs were burning and my thighs tight and cramped, the pain more exquisite than if you'd taken a paddle to my backside. Though it taught me never to bring you the wrong wine again.

The train slows, comes to a stop, and I feel a sick lurch in my stomach in response. We're so close to my destination, and now I'm going to be even later.

I'm not the only one who's biting back a groan of frustration, or glancing anxiously at a wristwatch. Most of my fellow passengers have already fired off text messages to explain their late arrival at wherever their destination might be. You don't allow me that luxury.

Could anyone in this carriage even begin to guess the

reason why I'm so twitchy, so desperate to be off the train? Surely not the man in the pinstripe suit opposite me, head buried in his evening paper. Though maybe he appreciates exactly what I'm going through; serious and sober, good-looking in his sleek silver-fox way, he strikes me as the type who may very well visit a mistress from time to time, grovelling at her feet in nothing but a pair of skimpy, see-through women's knickers and begging for the feel of her flogger on his bare, vulnerable arse.

Perhaps I'm reading him wrong, and he simply likes to watch. Would he get off on the sight of me bent over your whipping stool, panties yanked down round my knees and my wrists bound to the sturdy legs of the stool, so I can't pull away or rub my sore flesh as your cruel, thin cane comes down again and again?

Before I can fully engross myself in a fantasy where you punish me before an audience of leering middle-aged businessmen, wanking the cocks that jut from their flies as you thrash me till I'm a panting, tearful mess, the train starts moving again. A recorded voice kicks in, announcing that the next station is Barbican, and it's no illusion; we're clattering over the points, the platform coming into view. Pushing my way through the knot of commuters clustered by the doors, I make sure I'm first off the train. Normally, I'd show more in the way of courtesy, but I'm all too aware you're still waiting. My imagination can't help but picture you pacing the floor of your apartment in your riding boots, tapping a crop against your jodhpured thigh, and my pussy quivers in anticipation.

Taking the steps two at a time, passing through the ticket barrier whose gate moves far too slowly for my liking, I'm out on the street. Rain falls, heavy enough to warrant me reaching for my umbrella, but that takes time I don't have. For once, the traffic lights are kind, and I'm over the road, sprinting in the impractical heels I'd never have worn if I'd known I'd find myself racing to keep an appointment with you. But the point is I never know when you're going to call; as you always say, you like to keep me on my toes, rather than falling into some cosy, regular arrangement that dulls the edge of our master/slave relationship.

No one is around to pay me any attention as I trot through the small courtyard leading to the looming towers of the Barbican Estate. I stab at the doorbell and hear your answer almost immediately. 'Yes?'

'Sir, I'm sorry, I –'

'In the lift, girl. Now.' So it's not to be torture by stair-climbing this time, but that doesn't mean you're letting me off lightly. I know you too well to ever assume that.

As the lift ascends, I run my fingers through my dampened curls and glance at my reflection in the mirror of my compact. A pale, harassed face peers back at me and

I take a couple of deep breaths, centring myself – something I learned in a long-ago relaxation class. It calms the anxious pumping of my heart, but does nothing to release the erotic tension coiled so tightly in my belly. Even after the best part of two years together, that reaction still begins before I've even set eyes on you.

You answer the door almost before my knuckles rap against it. With a curt 'Inside', you usher me over the threshold, a fly stepping willingly into the spider's parlour.

'I take it there's a reason for your tardiness?' you say, not even glancing at me as I follow you through into the hall.

'Signal failure at Moorgate, sir. We were sitting outside Farringdon for ages.' The words sound woefully inadequate, but they seem to satisfy you for the time being.

'Can't be helped, I suppose, girl, but there are still consequences for being late, and I intend to make sure you appreciate them. Now, strip.'

This part of the routine never changes. You like me to be naked from the moment I step inside your apartment to the moment I leave. As I shrug off my coat, I take my first subtle glance at you. As always, the sight of you melts something inside me, setting off a rush of fierce, liquid heat. Dressed in your trademark black T-shirt, jodhpurs and those delicious shiny black riding boots, you're my every submissive dream made flesh. I might have been surrounded by dozens of better-looking men on the tube, but, though they might be taller than you, more athletically built, with thicker heads of hair and cheeks unmarked by the legacy of acne scars, they don't possess a fraction of your presence. They couldn't, as you do, issue an order that I'll obey without question, whether that's dropping any plans I might have made to be here before you, gradually peeling out of my boring work clothes, or inserting a pair of vibrating love balls into my cunt and wearing them throughout the course of an important meeting.

Jacket and skirt lie discarded on the polished floor-boards, and now my attention turns to my cream chain-store blouse. Like a butterfly emerging from a chrysalis, I'm stripping away the outer layers that mark me as an office drone, revealing the obedient submissive hidden within.

You don't say a word as I ease down my tights, careful not to snag them with a fingernail. Standing before you in mismatched bra and panties, it registers somewhere in my brain, as it always does at this moment, that there's something shameful about my eagerness to bare myself for you, to hand over just a little more control with every garment that comes off. We can't be equals, not when you're still fully dressed and I'm reaching behind me to unhook my bra, but it doesn't stop me. I want you to take control, to make me do whatever will satisfy your desire to punish me – a desire only matched by mine to take that punishment, to leave this apartment with the marks of your crop, your cane, your paddle on my skin.

I can't fight my instinct to delay the moment I expose my breasts as long as possible. They're too big, out of proportion on my small frame, and they sag more than I'd like. Revealing them has always made me feel self-conscious, however many times you've assured me you love them. Love to clamp them, bind them, too, but I don't think about that as I ease the straps off over my shoulders, holding the cups to my tits before finally dropping the bra on to the growing pile on the floor.

You say nothing, but your dark, intense gaze fixes on my nipples. Cool, uncritical scrutiny that makes the buds tighten, eager for the feel of fingers – or even those wicked bejewelled clamps – squeezing them to the point where pain and pleasure mesh.

Without a word, I hook my fingers in the waistband of my panties and take them down slowly, legs together, so that again you only get a flash of my pussy at the last possible moment. None of this shyness is feigned for your benefit; a little voice at the back of my head keeps up a running commentary, asking why it turns me on to be placed in such an embarrassing position. If I ever found the perfect answer to that question, this scene would lose much of its potency.

As it is, my underwear, soaked through at the crotch, joins the rest of my clothes, and you nod in satisfaction.

'Hands on your head, girl, and turn round slowly. Let me see everything.'

This is far from the most demeaning thing you could ask of me at this point. It's not unknown for you to order me to bend over and pull apart my arse cheeks, showing you the puckered hole hidden between them, and as I make a slow pirouette I'm still wondering when my real punishment for arriving half an hour late will kick in. Your next words make that a little clearer.

'Down on the floor. Crawl to the kitchen.'

Now you'll be able to see everything, as I shuffle on hands and knees through to the small kitchen, which is dominated by a huge American-style fridge. From the freezer compartment of that fridge, you order me to take out the bottle of vanilla vodka you store there. I'd hardly class it as the discerning dominant's drink of choice, but who am I to argue with your incongruous tastes?

As I pull open the freezer door, a blast of frigid air hits me, stiffening my nipples even further. I shiver as I reach for the bottle, and, though I can't see the amusement on your face, I know how much it entertains you to put me through this most subtle of torments. Once I've retrieved the vodka, I'm told to pour you a shot. You keep the glasses on a high shelf, and my breasts and bottom wobble as I reach up in ungainly fashion to bring one down. In normal circumstances, you'd offer me the use of a step stool to make the job easier, but these are hardly normal circumstances.

I hand the glass to you and wait for your approval. It comes in the form of a curt nod. Watching you drain the shot, I can almost taste its fiery bite, tempered by the sweetness of vanilla, but I won't be allowed a drink until the scene is over, and maybe not even then. You don't like anything to dull my reaction times, or my sensitivity to punishment.

Bottle stowed in the freezer once more, you order me to crawl to the guest room, following behind so you can savour the way my hanging breasts sway and slap together as I move.

You've told me so many times before how lucky you were to buy here at just the right time, before property prices skyrocketed and placed a two-bedroom apartment in this iconic development out of your reach. If anyone wondered why a single man might find it so necessary to have that extra space, they'd receive their answer the moment they stepped into this low-ceilinged, black-painted bedroom.

The picture window should offer a breathtaking view out over the City of London, but thick black-out curtains are pulled tight, completing the feeling of being utterly enclosed, cut off from the rest of the world. You told me, the first time I walked into this playroom, you'd had it extensively soundproofed. 'So scream as much as you like, girl. The neighbours will never hear you.'

Even though I've been in here so many times before, I can't help admiring the exquisite fittings that make it the perfect home dungeon. Now there's an idea for a magazine, I think, giggling despite the gravity of the situation. *Ideal Dungeon. This issue, Master X invites us to admire his lovely selection of antique tawses, and we let you know about the craftsman who'll build you a fully functional spit, no questions asked …*

Not that you have anything quite so outlandish here. Only the basics, but what beautiful basics they are: whipping stool, pillory and St Andrew's cross, all custom-made to your specifications. And on the far wall, neatly arranged, your extensive collection of punishment implements, from the lightest suede flogger to the heaviest Malacca cane. My back, my thighs, my bottom must have felt the impact of every single one.

'So, girl,' you murmur, half to yourself, 'what's it to be tonight?'

There's only one possible response to that question. 'Whatever you choose, sir.'

'Very good. The pillory, then.'

I hope you don't catch my quick smile. Of the three, it's the most comfortable to be placed in for any length of time, though all things are relative, naturally. You unlock it, raising the top part so I can place my wrists and head in the padded holes, before fastening it in place. The pillory forces me to stand with my rump thrust out, and I suspect that's the part of my body which will receive most attention tonight.

Almost sensing my train of thought, you say, 'So, you might be wondering why I chose the pillory? Well, I thought I'd teach you what happens when you're happy to simply sit on your backside, rather than making the effort to reach me on time.'

That's hardly a fair accusation, I want to reply, but nothing is fair in this game of punishment and reward. As my master, you can bend any rule, twist any statement to suit your perceptions. My next thought is that I'm glad I didn't confess to strap-hanging while I waited, or you'd have me straining on tiptoes to receive my punishment, wrists connected by a chain looped through one of the hooks screwed into the ceiling for exactly that purpose.

'As you were thirty minutes late, you're going to get thirty strokes, but I haven't yet decided on the implement. Your next answer is going to help me decide that. Tell me, girl, did anything that I might find significant happen to you on your way here?'

I think back, mentally retracing my journey. Nothing comes to mind at first, then the words tumble out, an unstoppable confession of the one thing you love above all else to punish me for.

'I – I started having a fantasy while I was waiting.'

'Really? Tell me more.'

'There was a businessman sitting opposite me on the train.' I don't mention my initial assessment of the man as a fellow sub; that isn't what you want to hear. 'I was thinking what it would be like if you punished me in front of him. In my mind, he had his cock out and was wanking it while you caned me.' Sensing your excitement, I pick up the scenario and run with it. 'You'd get my arse all red and sore, then you'd encourage him to shoot his come over the marks you'd left, so I could feel it running down my crack. Or maybe you'd make me suck him off. He'd have a big cock, so big it stretched my mouth, and you'd encourage him to thrust hard down my throat, so he was fucking my face, and he wouldn't stop till he'd shot every drop of his spunk and I'd had to swallow it all down.'

You're standing behind me, so I can't see your face – or your cock, though I'm sure it's hard in your tight-fitting jodhpurs. I've never yet been punished in front of an audience, but you keep telling me one day it will happen, and now I barely have a fantasy where there isn't some third party, male or female, watching and joining in my subjugation. Just thinking about it now has my juices flooding from me, wetting the tops of my thighs.

'Interesting,' you say at length. 'Well, that's made up

my mind for me. I'd been torn between using three implements – the crop, the flogger and the rubber paddle. That
little confession has convinced me I don't need to choose.
You're getting ten strokes of each.'

That sounds bearable. Then you decide to raise the
stakes a little higher.

'You're deciding the order in which I use them. Give
me the numbers one to three, in any order.'

Without thinking about it, I reply, 'Two, three, one.'

'Very good. You've chosen the paddle first, then the
crop, then the flogger.'

I should have known you'd rank them from lightest
to most severe. As it is, I'll have to endure ten with the
paddle. It's not the most painful thing you could use, but
repeated blows build a sustained, dull ache, impossible
to ignore. Follow that with the sharp sting of the crop
and – well, I'll deal with that when it happens.

'Are you ready, girl?'

'Yes, sir.'

That's the last word you speak before my punishment
begins. You don't ask me to count the strokes, or thank
you between them; that part of the ritual has never
appealed. My gasps and cries are more than enough
acknowledgement that your blows are having the desired
effect.

A light tap on each cheek with the paddle gives me a
moment to get used to its weight, to anticipate how it

will feel when it slams down hard. My mouth dries; even the slow, measured breathing that calmed me on the way up to your apartment is ineffective now.

You space the ten strokes out, letting me almost but not quite recover from each before dishing out the next. At first, I bear the pain almost in silence, but, as the brutal, bruising blows continue to fall, that becomes impossible. By eight, I'm whimpering and, by ten, I'm responding with a full-throated yell.

'Very good, girl.'

Your hand smoothes over my arse, which already feels hot and swollen, and we're barely a third of the way through. The pillory, like all the other pieces of furniture in the room, is positioned so I'm staring at the rack of punishment implements. It gives me the perfect view as you replace the paddle and take down the crop.

This is your signature implement, the one you wield with the greatest relish. It slashes down against my exposed flanks, leaving a burning stripe of pain in its wake, and I give in to my urge to shriek and stamp my feet, begging you to stop. But you show me no mercy, and once the crop has done its wicked work there's still the flogger to come.

Now your truly sadistic side comes to the fore. The ten lashes of the flogger are directed at the soft, delicate flesh of my inner thighs. The soft suede tails flail in unison, moving closer to my pussy lips, and I fear you'll actually aim the last strokes at my most tender places, striking my clit. You spare me that torment but, by the time you finish, my face is as blotchy as my backside, streaked with tears, and I know I've been on the receiving end of a thorough beating.

'Well done, girl,' you croon, as you free me from the pillory, taking me in your arms and cradling me so you can brush the wet strands of hair from my face and rain soft kisses on my cheeks.

Your finger pushes its way between my legs, parting the soft folds of my sex and burrowing into my core. As I cling to you, thanking you for punishing me so beautifully, you circle my clit, teasing caresses that have my thighs lolling apart, offering you easier access. After the pain you've inflicted, the pleasure of your touch is all the sweeter, and I close my eyes, giving in to the orgasm that pulses through me.

I could take more of this treatment, letting peak rise on peak till I'm spent, but there'll be time for that later. Now, you urge me down to my knees, letting your cock free from the constricting embrace of your jodhpurs.

My tongue flicks over the smooth, salty crown, striking the cold metal of your Prince Albert piercing. This is how I love to thank you for punishing me, and I gradually take more of you in my mouth.

'So, now you know what happens when you're late, girl,' you say, grunting with the satisfaction of being lodged securely in my throat, 'I trust you'll be punctual in future?'

In all honesty, it's not a promise I can give; after all, I thought I'd be on time today and the transport system conspired to prevent that happening. All I can tell you is that I'll try, and if I happen to be late again – well, I'll trust you to deal with me in the stern, authoritarian, loving way only you can.

Life Begins at Forty
Primula Bond

I'm forty today. I've come home as usual to an empty house. No one to show off my new dress to. No one greeting me at the door with a cake, some new perfume or tickets to a show. Oh, I'll be going out at the weekend. My friend Lucy has arranged some kind of get-together, but not even she knows my exact age because to me it only marks forty years of making stupid mistakes.

I dump my shopping bags full of comfort treats on my sparkling new breakfast bar. Bottles of sauvignon blanc, ready-made coronation chicken, raspberries and cream, and a vast bar of Belgian chocolate. I run the bath and fill it with oils and bubbles while I take off my clothes in front of the mirror to take a good look. Three stone less of me since I hit thirty-nine. Nice, straight white teeth. Nose a little neater. A new woman, really.

It may all sound a bit solitary and sad but there's no need to feel too sorry for me. This is bliss compared with this time last year, a birthday which was far more traumatic than this one. Mooching peacefully round my lovely flat tonight, a few irons in the fire for the weekend, food, drink, a great DVD to watch later, believe me, it's all good.

The night of my last birthday was the night my fiancé chose to leave me. Gave no clue, no reason for his betrayal. Just fell out of love, I guess, though Lucy and the others all reckon there must have been another woman. Either way, I came home that night and he had literally vanished without trace.

Maybe what he saw back then was the old, fat me who'd let herself go and took him for granted. But the irony is there's nothing like sheer misery for losing weight, which leads to an unintentional make-over. So what he was missing was my new body, wardrobe full of size 10s, a different hairstyle, all topped off with a touch of Botox here and there. Basically he was missing the new me.

But the worst thing was I never knew what frustration felt like until he left. Does anyone know how many calories you burn stroking yourself to a frenzy night after night?

I've been celibate since he left, unless you count my

Rampant Rabbit. I rejected the idea of internet dating, though I did try a speed-dating night once. But I was still fat then. Lucy came with me, just for a dare, and she pulled some bloke, but I didn't.

I even took the plunge and went for an interview at an older women's escort agency, though I never told Lucy this. They were very enthusiastic about taking me on, actually. Loved my curves, they said. My big mournful eyes and juicy lips. The extra weight was attractive to many men, they said. And they were so keen that they sent me then and there on a date with a very large, very rich businessman called Colin who had a moustache and spent dinner ogling my cleavage, then pawing at my breasts in his hotel room, then when I undid my blouse for him he nuzzled into my bosom and started sucking my nipples – to fulfil his mummy fantasy, I suppose, but that was fine by me and I was really getting turned on.

I'd never been sucked by a man with a moustache and its stiff hair rubbing on the skin of my breast was weirdly mind-blowing, like some kind of furry animal nibbling at me, but bizarrely he wouldn't let me touch him, wouldn't let me near his fly or his cock or anything, so while he was sucking away at me I grabbed his hand and pushed it between my legs and made him rub up and down over my pussy which made him buck and groan and bite me all the harder, and it was pretty pervy in a good way. In fact, I was on the point of coming when his mobile phone buzzed underneath me. It was his wife, and that was the end of that.

'It's time to move on,' Lucy says to me frequently. 'Anyway, we're all sick and tired of hearing how that bastard was the love of your life.'

Not Colin, obviously. She means Jamie. And she's right. I've bored everyone rigid with my misery. So this year my new body and I intend to enjoy ourselves. It would be a waste of all this super subtle work, otherwise. These slim, toned legs want to open and wrap around a man. These big bouncy breasts want a man's, or men's, lips to suck them. But men aren't handed to you on a plate, are they?

Lucy means well, but she's always busy with her own life, dropping in and out of mine when she smells a party. She'll never understand how he broke my heart.

Tonight I want to be alone. I dim the lights, just have Miles Davis serenading me. Then I slip into the bath with a sigh, sinking into the whispering bubbles.

A man on a plate. How would that be? My legs fall open as I imagine him. My toes curl round the taps as I try to picture him, but he always has Jamie's face. I want him to stride into the bathroom, heave me out of the water, throw me down on the cold hard floor and fuck me right there, all wet and slippery.

The foam covers each breast. I push them upwards through the bubbles and my nipples harden. I can be proud of them again. Jamie used to love sucking them. I used to wear tight, low tops, until they got so big that I looked like a cheap barmaid. But, even when they were huge, Jamie still used to rip at my clothes, fondle my tits, scrape his chin over my soft skin and bite on my nipples until desire rose and blossomed inside me and I screeched at him to do it to me, wherever we were.

But even while he was fucking me back then, only a year ago, he must have been planning his escape. Maybe he was finding me so repellent he had to think of someone else while we were at it, someone slimmer and more confident. Someone like the old me.

I can feel desire seething in me now as I part my legs under the water, find my hand soaping my pussy. I push myself upwards in the water. My tits are like cream cakes, the nipple a dark cherry popping on top. That reminds me. Food.

As I'm sinking lower in the water, my fingers crawling up inside me now, I think I can hear the front door banging. My eyes snap open, heart thudding. As I rise like a mermaid out of the water, everything, the steam, the tiles, the taps, swims before me. I wrap a towel round me and pad out into the living room, feeling faint from the too-hot water. The towel grazes my still hard nipples. No sign of anyone. Must have been the wind. Back to the bath?

I reach for the light switch. No. Candles would be

better. Thick church candles. Always soothing, guaranteed to keep up this level of sensuality. I want more atmosphere. It's my birthday, for God's sake. Let me revel. Let me think about that imaginary man on a plate if I want to, and touch myself while I fantasise.

I go into the kitchen. The raspberries are heaped in a glass bowl and I'm going to eat my meal backwards, pudding first. I pour cream all over them, sprinkle loads of sugar, and wander back into the sitting room, with the bowl and the chilled wine.

The candle flames grow tall, measuring their own shadows on the wall. They glow on the mirror and fill the room with a warm glow. My reflection looks sexy, wet from the bath, towel slipping down, lips big and glistening with wanting.

In the mirror is my sitting room. The big white sofas, re-covered when I had the place done up after Jamie left. Pristine. No stain of him or our endless fucking sessions left on the upholstery. There are my photographs, hanging from my last exhibition, including one of him. I put it into the show, even though it hurts every time I look at it, because it's my masterpiece. He's posing like Michelangelo's David but instead of being planted in Florence he was standing on Primrose Hill, looking over London.

And there's my Persian rug, also cleaned since he left. I nearly drop the bowl of raspberries and the wine.

Because also reflected there, as if it's been growing out of the floor while I've been in the bath, is a giant birdcage.

It's beautifully constructed. All wrought iron in waves and curves, glinting in some places, in others almost melting away in a lacy mesh. And there's a little grille for a door. And it's locked.

I wrench open the front door. No one on the pavement outside my house. Lucy has a key for when I'm away, but that's all.

I look at the cage. There's a shape humped inside, but I can't make out what it is. Might be some kind of wild animal, and if this is supposed to be a gift then it's backfired, because I hate dogs, cats, birds. Lions and tigers for that matter.

Or maybe it's meant as a prop or ornament for my tropical plant collection. Lucy knows how much I want to buy a Venus flytrap.

I creep closer, bend down to look. A little label pinned to the door says, simply, 'slave'. My neck prickles with fear. And weird excitement. I put down the bottle and the bowl of raspberries. Cream is dripping over the edge.

There's no wild animal here. No exotic plant. No psychedelic bird. Inside the cage there is a man. Totally naked. Rocked back on his haunches and staring through the bars at me.

The towel slips right off as my hands fly to my mouth.

The cool air brushes over me. My breasts swell from my ribcage as I screech out. He silently looks my body up and down. The damp skin round my nipples shrinks back, making the hard buds poke out. I glance to see if he's locked in. Or can I get him out?

His eyes are beautiful. So dark. Mouth unsmiling. Shoulders bunched as he grasps the bars of his cage. He's as still as a statue, waiting for a gesture from me. If he's the slave, does that make me the mistress? My stomach goes tight with the thought of it. My eyes go straight down between his legs, at the line of hair leading down from his chest into the thicket of dark hair. At his big bare cock resting there, twitching once, twice as I stare at it, then rising slowly.

I get down on my hands and knees and crawl towards the cage. I yank open the door. What was I saying earlier about waste? My heart is thudding so hard my breasts are wobbling. Still he doesn't move. I open my mouth to speak, shut it again. Instead, I sit back on my own haunches, mirroring his position, and silently crook my finger.

He crawls out, halting just in front of me. The candles flicker as we move slightly. His cock hangs under his belly, like he's a raging bull or something. My ragged breathing is giving me away, not to mention my nipples hard as nuts. I grab him by the hair and pull him nearer me.

'Hungry?'

He nods, trying to grab at me. I shake my head, pull away. Instead, I point to the bowl of raspberries on the floor.

'So eat.'

He puts his head into the bowl like a pussycat and starts to munch at the raspberries. I try not to gasp with laughter. I can't believe he's actually doing this.

'You'll do anything I say, then?'

He nods, looking up. Raspberry juice trickles down his chin. Cream is caught in the crease above his mouth. I scoop up a handful of raspberries too, cram them into my mouth, lick and chew and swallow. I lick my lips, all clean.

'Then touch me.'

We're facing each other like two praying figures. I straighten up to be higher than him, and guide his hands up my sides. Up to my waiting, aching breasts. They quiver as I try to control my breath. I'm trying so hard to look cool, take it slow, but my head is rushing with all that suppressed desire, a year of stupid, frustrating celibacy. Christ, I'm already wet between my legs and it's not from bathwater.

I scoop up some cream, my throat tight with desire as I dab thick dollops on to each nipple.

'Suck me.'

I make him push my breasts together so that my nipples are side by side, hard points covered in thick cream and angled towards his mouth. I squash myself against him, suffocating him with my breasts, pressing them over his cheeks and ears.

His lips graze each nipple, then his tongue flicks out in circles round the edge, over the puckered skin. Licking the cream off to get to the sore tip. His hands knead my breasts hard enough to hurt, and I don't stop him. Just press harder against him. At last when he's licked off the cream his teeth close over one nipple while his fingers tweak and pinch the other, then he's biting and nipping at both of them. I hold his head tight inside my cleavage.

My whole body is shivering with frustration and desire. I take another handful of raspberries and cream and push him down on his back. I smear the pudding into my pussy and crawl over him until I am hovering above his face. I feel his breath whispering on the skin inside my thighs, feel his big hands taking my legs and parting them, and then I lower myself so that my pussy is in his face. I nearly scream out loud when his tongue comes out and swipes up my cunt, warm and wet, licking the cream off my lips, off the little frills inside, nudging into the crack to get at my throbbing clit. My buttocks jerk backwards. I want to rub myself over his face and come, I'm so close to it already, but I can't let it happen yet, he's here at my mercy and I can use him whichever way I want, but here it comes and I can't help it, his tongue pushes inside me and my cunt grips it and the climax swells and breaks, and I come, grinding and panting, all over his face.

I lie on top of him, shivering with cold and lust and excitement, and wonder if I've used up all my credit in one go.

He lies totally still, just licking the rest of the cream off his mouth. He's not going anywhere. I know how to relight this fire. It never fails. I rouse myself after a few minutes and move myself back so that he can take my tits into his mouth again. It always works. It's like having an electric shock. How have I done without this kind of attention all this time?

I straddle him, wedging his face against my breasts, pushing hard at him so that he bites my nipples and hurts me. As he suckles me, I wrap my slim, newly toned legs round his hips and pull my wet pussy into his groin. I'm already close to frenzy with all his sucking and fondling, raspberry juice and cream making me sticky. I inch closer, not yet touching his dick, so that it's buried between us, its swollen head nudging my stomach. On impulse I reach into the bowl of raspberries again and without looking down I smear fruit and cream all over his cock, cupping his balls in my hand before smearing them with the mess as well.

It's been a year. It's time to do something I've never done before. I've always loved eating, but what about using food for fucking?

'Now fuck me, lover.'

I tilt my hips to guide his cock inside. He grips me with one strong arm to keep me steady. But the first few inches slip easily inside, filling me with cock and raspberry and cream, and it's so sticky and wicked, the sugar grating on the tender flesh and making a rough friction as his cock travels further inside. My cunt tightens and grips round it like a greedy mouth and I fall forward, impaled on several more rigid inches of his cock. The raspberries and cream and sugar sting and irritate me deliciously all the way up inside me. He falls, and I push him down on to his back.

The sight of him lying beneath me, his hands still holding my dangling breasts, mouth and teeth still nibbling and licking, the feel of the pips and sticky juice and my own wetness and cream dribbling out of me drives me down on to him sooner than I intended. My bottom slams against his balls and desire fans like wildfire through me till I think I'm going mad.

I force myself to pull away, slide back up the length like a flag up a pole, hover on the end of it, tense my thighs for a moment of suspense, smear just cream on to me this time, just rub it in over my sex lips and over what I can see of his cock, lovely and smooth and cool, then I slowly grind down again until the length of him is swallowed up inside me.

'That's it, baby. I said, fuck me!'

I sound like Madonna, the way she half talks, half sings so filthily in her song 'Erotica'. Jamie and I used to listen to and dance to Madonna. We went to her concerts. I even dressed up as her when I was younger. She and I have grown up together, side by side. She's the raunchy elder sister I never had, showing me the way. I even have my hair dyed blonde, like hers, described in Hollywood as the colour of a dirty pillow slip.

Now I let my slave have his way. I let him thrust. I couldn't stop him if I tried, and it's time he did some work. It feels as if he's going to slam right through my head. I've waited so long for this. We get into rhythm and we burn together, our breath making the candles flicker wildly. As we go faster I hear a low, surprised groaning from him. His head falls back on the carpet.

'Whoever brought you here,' I whisper, riding him slowly, bending so that my nipples dangle in his face, 'did they tell you what to expect? Did they promise you it would be this good?'

He smiles then, the corner of his mouth catching in his teeth. 'It's much, much better.'

I grind back down and start to ride him, bucking hard, cream oozing out of me, moaning as the ecstasy comes closer, tears burning as I look down at him. He's panting like a dog, that lovely groaning getting more desperate. He's totally under my power. He couldn't resist me or disobey if he tried.

I almost laugh out loud with it, and as I buck wildly and start to come and his helpless male groans fill my ears I bend down to kiss him, lick his lips, flick my tongue over his teeth, suck his slippery tongue and then the kiss makes me come in a great rush and I call out for my slave, over and over again.

He strains up beneath me, his cock pumping his life juice into me. I squeeze everything out of him, never wanting it to end. Although of course the sooner it ends, the sooner it can begin again.

The crazy jerking slows down to stillness and our moans turn to quiet breathing. I slide off his softening cock. My legs unfold and I lie down beside him on the rug, spunk and cream and raspberry juice all over my thighs. He licks them and my pussy clean like a giant cat, making me arch and writhe. I can't believe I want him again already. The jazz in the background dies to one solitary note.

He lies back on the rug, quiet, tame. Totally mine. I'm weakening. He's so gorgeous.

'Better now?'

He smiles and rises up on his elbow, reaches towards the cold bottle of wine. There's plenty of time. We have all night. There's no meter on his cage as far as I can see. I can keep him as long as I like. I jump up, wrap the towel firmly round me again. I'm shaking, actually. It's like he's unlocked me. Forget coronation chicken and raspberries. It's him I want to eat.

But for now I tilt the bottle of wine straight into my mouth, swallow, and wipe my mouth crudely.

'Get back inside.'

I point at the cage. He doesn't move. He's like a god lying there. I shove him with my foot. He heaves himself up on his hands and knees. Not so humble now. But I shake my head, smothering my smile, and slap him on the backside. He jerks and groans but he's grinning as well. I smack him again, watching the red handprints come up on his buttock, the arching of his back and the flexing of the muscles down his sides as he relishes the sensation. I want to go on and on with this. Then I want him to smack me.

But I must play the role of mistress properly, and for a little longer.

He waits for more, but I kick him right into the cage and lock the little door, waving the key in front of his face.

'So. Whose idea was this birthday present? Where have you been?'

I lower the towel, press myself against the bars so my nipples squeeze through, tease my hand down between my legs. His tired cock lifts a little.

'Ask Lucy,' he mumbles, inching closer to flick at my nipple with his tongue.

'That bitch!' I am red-hot with anger.

'No, no. This was your birthday present!'

50

'Maybe, but it's all making sense now. Getting me out of the way that night you buggered off. Vanishing herself for several weeks with no explanation. Always going on about what happened, even when I was trying to get over it. Boy, is she going to pay for this!'

'I think this was supposed to make up for all that.'

I glance at another photograph, this time on the mantelpiece. A handsome, laughing guy, the corner of his mouth caught in his teeth.

'Happy birthday, darling,' says Jamie softly, kneeling up in his cage. 'You look so good, you know. Ten years younger.'

I can't resist him. I never could.

'What the hell. I'll punish her later.' I wrench open the door. 'But for now, well, life begins at forty, eh?'

And I pull him out, and he falls on top of me, and I laugh, because we're going to do it all over again.

Thawing Ms Frost
Kat Black

The redhead in the razor-cut skirt suit ends the predinner staff meeting with a simple sharp turn of her heel. Heading off in the direction of the kitchens and the office beyond, her strides cut through the heavy stillness left hanging over the dining room.

Leaning against the front of the lacquered cherrywood bar, arms crossed over his white-shirted chest, Café Cluny's new barman watches her go, gaze sliding from the tightly rolled twist of her hair, past the purposeful swing of her hips, and all the way down to the soles of her spiked black stilettos.

So – he whistles under his breath – that's my boss. And, from first impressions, she lives up to every word of warning he's heard from his colleagues over the past week. Even fresh back from a fortnight's holiday, Annabel Frost seems about as chilled as an Arctic icicle.

She's stunning too, with that ruby-red dye job and matching lipstick giving her a vibrant appearance so at odds with the frosty personality. Judging by her ivory complexion and green eyes, he bets there's a natural redhead lurking beneath the chemically enhanced one.

It isn't until the kitchen door swings closed behind her that he's pulled from his reverie by a sudden collective sigh of relief hissing around him like so many punctured tyres.

'The Bitch is back,' he hears one of the commis chefs mutter, as the starched-white huddle of kitchen staff head off back towards their shiny steel domain.

Tim, one of the waiters, moves up to the bar beside him and claps a supportive hand on his shoulder. 'Told you so.'

Sweet-natured Donna comes up as well, taking advantage of the situation to lay a shyly suggestive hand on his forearm. 'She had no right to talk to you that way, Aidan.' She looks up at him through her lashes. 'You mustn't let her get you down.'

'Not a problem,' Aidan assures her, straightening and moving away.

As lovely and as willing as Donna is, her gentle femininity does nothing for him. Taking up his station behind the bar, he wonders what her delicate sensibilities would make of the fact that, far from getting him down, the arbitrary tongue-lashing he'd just received from his new boss left him not only well and truly up, but also hard and throbbing inside his uniform black trousers.

Returning to the task of slicing lemons, he bows his head, letting the unruly fall of his hair hide his smile as he contemplates what a pleasure it's going to be dragging the haughty Ms Frost off her high horse and teaching her to enjoy kneeling at his feet. Especially if she insists on kicking and screaming against him every inch of the way, as he's certain she will.

***

From her position at the lectern-style front desk, Annabel sweeps her gaze over the packed restaurant, checking that everything in her world is running as it should: staff busy but polite, service efficient, customers happy.

Cluny's is popular, and tonight the atmosphere is as sparkling as ever, with the background strains of easy jazz overlaid by the lively buzz of chatter and punctuated by the chink of cutlery against china.

Satisfied, she casts her eye over the bar area, only to discover the new dark-haired barman – Andy or Adam or something – looking back at her. It's not the first time this evening she's caught him staring, not the first time she's felt a spurt of irritation at the cocky, vaguely amused glint in his eyes.

Already beyond annoyed to have come back to work to find that a replacement for the previous no-hoper had been drafted in without her approval, Annabel decides that enough is enough. She lays her fountain pen along the open spine of the reservations book and starts off in the direction of the bar. Time to teach the new boy his place.

'Is there a problem over here?' she demands, stepping into the narrow area between the polished bar and the mirror-backed wall of shelves displaying an impressive array of bottles. 'Only you seem to be spending an awful lot of time standing around staring into space instead of working.'

Rather than snapping to attention and spewing excuses and apologies as she expects, the tall, rangy man takes a moment to wipe his hands on a towel. 'You know very well that I've been working, Annabel,' he says with a soft, southern Irish lilt and a crooked smile that belie the intense focus of the blue gaze he sweeps over the spotless and organised area. After folding the towel by the sink, he turns that gaze on her and saunters her way. 'Just like you know that "space" isn't what I've been looking at.'

Unused to being answered back by her staff, Annabel feels her eyes widen with surprise at his audacity. It takes only a moment to recompose herself. 'It's Ms Frost, actually. And I have to say I don't like your attitude.'

'Well, now.' He keeps walking towards her until he's right up close and lowers his face and voice so that only the two of them can hear. 'That makes two of us, because I don't think much of yours, either.'

She nearly chokes. None of her staff have ever had the nerve to speak to her in such a way. 'I beg your pardon?' She tries not to splutter. 'You can't talk to me like that, I'm your manager.'

'Oh, I know who you are, sweetheart. You're all I've been thinking about for the past three hours.' His eyes trace the contours of her face. 'What do you look like with that glorious hair let loose? Will you wear it down for me tomorrow?'

'What? No!' Annabel flounders, completely wrong-footed by his forward insolence. 'I don't know what working environment you're used to, but here your behaviour is inappropriate. If you persist, I'll have no option but to instigate disciplinary measures.'

'You'll punish me?' he asks without a hint of concern but with an infuriating tease of a smile. Breaking off, he spears a straw each into a couple of mojitos sweating on a tray and pushes the lot towards an incoming waiter. Once they're alone again, he returns his attention to her. 'Would that make you wet?'

Annabel can feel her mouth moving, but there are no

words to come out. The man is un-be-liev-able. And that swooping sensation low down in her belly is nothing but righteous anger.

'No,' he answers his own question, tilting his head his head to the side. 'Despite the dominatrix image you like to portray, I don't think that's your style.' His eyes narrow as he studies her. 'Now, maybe if I were to punish *you* …?'

Shocked by his lewd talk but unwilling to cause a public scene, Annabel spins away to face the shelves, pretending to straighten a row of already perfectly aligned hi-ball tumblers to give herself a moment to gather her flustered wits. In an instant, he is right there behind her, his proximity making her skin prickle.

'Is that a blush I see staining those cheeks? Lovely.' His voice is a satisfied murmur and his breath whispers against the spot behind her ear, stirring the tiniest of hairs. 'I bet you blush when you come, too. Bet that pure white skin flushes rosy all the way down to your chest. Am I right, Annabel? I've been trying to picture it, you know – how you'll look when I drive you to that moment of surrender.'

Before she can stop the instinctive reaction, she gasps and her gaze flicks up to meet his in the mirror. He stands so close, taller by half a head, the width of his shoulders blocking her view of the busy room behind him. She should move away, put a stop to this blatant sexual harassment, but she feels so unsteady that all she can do is grasp at the counter top for support.

'I've been getting hard just wondering if you're the type to cry out loud, or gasp and bite your lip. Whether you tremble and shake all the way down to your toes, or bow in a rigid, graceful arch.' The light in his eyes is fierce, fascinating, frightening. 'Will you come all over my cock in a rush, or a slow, creamy ooze?'

Annabel shakes her head in mute, desperate denial of his words and, more worryingly, the rush of excitement they kindle deep inside her.

Ignoring the plea, he keeps their gazes locked and leans forward, trickling the words 'I'm going to strip you naked and find out' into her ear with no trace of a question, no doubt in his tone, just implacable certainty. 'Soon.'

'Er, excuse me. Ms Frost, Aidan?' Donna's voice intrudes from behind.

Turning as her tormentor steps back, Annabel sees the diminutive waitress standing on the other side of the bar, a little crease between her brows as she looks between them.

'Sorry, I – I need a bottle of Rioja and three sparkling waters for table nine.'

'Right away, sweetheart.' Aidan's voice is pitched in its cordial Irish tone – at least until he turns and reaches around Annabel to retrieve the glasses. 'Don't be forgetting about the hair tomorrow,' he whispers before moving away to fill the order.

Senses reeling, Annabel makes a dash for freedom and steers well clear of him for the rest of the service.

* * *

Of course, the lovely Ms Frost doesn't disappoint him, turning up for her next shift with her hair pulled into the tightest bun Aidan has ever seen, which leaves her barely able to blink.

Even the fuck-off-and-die scowl she sends him in return for his amused smile is hampered, but not enough for him to mistake it for anything but what it is.

She's careful to keep away from him, sticking to the dining area and harrying the wait staff. Given the amount of time she spends sneaking little glances his way and chewing at that ruby-red bottom lip when she thinks no one is looking, Aidan knows that keeping her distance won't do her the slightest bit of good.

The dinner crowd has cleared down to the last two tables of espresso-and-brandy stragglers by the time he looks up to see her stalking towards the bar with an all-business jut to her chin.

'Aidan,' she begins with her nose in the air, keeping the solid barrier of cherrywood between them.

He hides his pleasure at hearing her use his name for the first time and ponders how thrilling it's going to be to hear her call him 'sir'. He places the last dirty glass in the washer and straightens. 'Annabel?'

He notices the slight flinch she tries to contain at his familiar form of address. Half of him hopes she'll dare to demand that he call her 'Ms Frost' so he can get her face-down over his knee before the night is through. Those veiled looks of hers have been searing his nerves all service. He flexes his right hand as his palm tingles with anticipation.

Something of his thoughts must show, because she swallows and refrains from correcting him.

'I'm sure that, on reflection, you'll agree your behaviour last night was unprofessional and unacceptable.' She pauses, expecting his agreement. When he remains silent, those red lips tighten.

'However,' she resumes, 'I've decided to take into consideration the fact that you're new here, and, as long as you're prepared to apologise and give me your assurance that you'll never behave in such a personally offensive manner again, I'll agree to put the entire episode behind us.'

Prepared speech over, Annabel Frost faces him down, presenting an outward demeanour that could freeze the balls off a brass monkey. If he wasn't standing directly opposite her and didn't know what to look for, he'd miss the rapid flicker of the pulse point at the base of her throat telling him she isn't feeling quite as composed as she looks. Inwardly, she's either mad as hell, scared to her marrow or reluctantly aroused – he's willing to put his money on a thrilling mix of all three.

'I can't do that,' he tells her.

She stiffens and blinks. 'Why not?' There's a ring of challenge in her tone but he sees that flicker begin to accelerate.

'Because I refuse to apologise for something I found so enjoyable, Annabel. And I won't be made a liar by promising not to do it again when I have every intention of doing precisely that. It's too much fun watching you get your tight white panties in a knot.'

And that puts the first real crack in Annabel Frost's tightly held control. There's a flash of temper in her green eyes before she narrows them and grits her teeth. 'I've just told you not to talk to me that way. Leave my underwear out of it!'

'Great idea. Come in tomorrow without any – a pair of lacy-topped stockings is all you'll need under that skirt. I've been dying to see what colour curls you're hiding between your legs.'

Her eyes snap wide and her face heats red. 'You're perverted!' she hisses.

'Why, thank you, Ms Frost.'

'And disgusting,' she spits, although the rapid rise and fall of her chest pushing her hard-tipped breasts against her shirt and that flush staining her cheeks say she's anything but repulsed.

'Careful now,' he warns her gently. 'Insults will only get you punished.'

'You wouldn't dare lay a finger on me,' she huffs.

'Oh, I'd dare to use more than a finger,' he parries, enjoying the clash of wills. 'There's a whole world of erotic torment I'd like to introduce you to, Annabel.'

'You might find that difficult,' she snipes, but he detects the underlying tremble in her tone. 'Seeing as I'll never let you touch me.'

He flashes her a knowing smile. 'Now here's the funny thing.' He leans forward over the bar as though to tell her a secret. 'I don't need to touch you to make you mine. Soon, all I'll have to do is look at you across the room to make you gasp and shiver and know you belong to me.'

'Don't be so ridiculous.' Despite her bravado, she backs up an inch. 'I'm not yours and never will be.'

He straightens, changing his smile to one of 'if you say so', which infuriates his sparring partner to the point that he can almost hear her mentally stomping her foot.

'Why are you doing this?' she demands, unable to hide the snap of petulance in her tone that shoots straight to his right palm and groin.

'Apart from wanting to fuck you inside out? Because I sense a need in you that I understand and know how to fulfil.'

His raw language causes her to flinch, but she's quick to rally and stand her ground. 'How presumptuous.'

'I'm a good judge of character, Annabel.'

'Really? Well, do share your expertise and tell me what this supposed *need* is, then.'

He pauses for a moment, watching her bristle. 'All this attitude.' He sweeps a hand up and down, the gesture encompassing her from head to toe. 'And the hard-nosed face you present to the world, it's just a cover to hide your true nature, to bury the desires you're too afraid to admit to.' He can see a spark of wariness in her eyes, sense her bracing herself, ready for denial and defence. 'That yearning you have to surrender control, the need you feel to be cuffed and collared and taken in hand.'

For a split second her eyes are huge and fearful, telling him he's spot on. God, that flash of sweet vulnerability shoots a bolt of fire down the stiffened shaft of his cock, and makes him want to bend her over the bar right now and fuck her hard until she's delirious with pleasure.

'A doormat?' she spits. 'That's what you think I am?' The laugh she gives is hollow and contemptuous. 'You must be blind.'

'I can see perfectly, thanks – right though the bratty façade to the strong, independent, capable woman beneath. Doormats don't do it for me.'

'And arsehole misogynist control freaks don't do it for me. Sounds like a terminal case of incompatibility.'

'Now that's where you're wrong. If you think I don't know that your nipples are hard and those tightie-whities are hot and damp between your thighs because of what we're doing here, think again.'

She looks about ready to explode – with heat, and anger, and frustration. And he knows once again he's right.

'Insufferable bastard,' she mutters under her breath.

'I've given you fair warning, Annabel.' It's the first time he's used his 'Dom' voice, and he notes that the stern tone isn't lost on her. 'You ever speak to me like that again and I'll come at you. And regardless of where or when or who's watching, I *will* put my hands on you then and leave you in no doubt as to who belongs to whom.'

She gapes at him, luscious lips doing the same cute little fish impression they did yesterday as she tries and fails to find her voice. For once she seems to consider retreat the better part of valour. Spinning away, she flees to safety, but not before Aidan's noted the darkening of those green eyes as her pupils dilate with desire.

* * *

Annabel is beyond relieved to find the bar area devoid of antagonistic Irish libertines when she arrives the next day, much later than usual, and busy pretending that her tardiness has nothing to do with avoidance tactics.

Making her way through the kitchens, she barely

registers the sudden exaggerated burst of activity – a sight that should fill her with satisfaction but today highlights the extent of her distraction.

With an angry shove at the fire door leading to the staff loos and office, she determines to pull herself together. No way is she going to let some kinky son-of-a-bitch barman undermine the authority and control she's worked so long and hard to –

She freezes in the act of pushing open the office door, her grip tightening on the handle as she notices the internal door leading to the cellar is ajar. Her gaze flicks instantly to the filing cabinet where the spare set of keys is hidden, registering the open drawer. Obvious sounds of movement and a stream of appreciative, accented mutterings float up the stairs.

Her simmering temper flashes to a hot, fast boil. Bloody man! She should have known. Releasing the door, which swings closed behind her, she marches across the small room and shouts, 'What the hell are you doing down there?'

'Annabel, hello. I was thinking maybe you weren't coming in today.'

She curls her hands into fists and starts stomping down the stairs. 'What do you think you're doing? The cellar is off limits to unsupervised staff. How did you find the key?'

'Ah, well, the boss phoned to say he's coming in tonight

with a table of friends he's wanting to impress. As you weren't in, he told me about his private collection here and where to find the key.'

By the light of the single bare bulb hanging from the cobwebbed rafters, Annabel spots the bane of her life as she steps down on to the dusty concrete floor. Just the sight of his back turned towards her as he fiddles about at the bench against the far wall has her hands itching to reach out and – what? Strike him? Caress him?

She shakes her head to clear the confusing thought. 'Well, I'm here now,' she snaps. 'So you can leave it with me and get back upstairs to the bar.'

'Actually, I'm all done.' He turns and strides towards her holding a tray laden with bottles. 'I just need you to take this for a minute.' He pushes the tray towards her so quickly her hands have grasped it before she's registered what's happening.

'There, now be very careful with that. The Louis XIII Cognac alone is worth about £1,300. Add the rest and we're looking at in excess of three grand's worth of rare booze. Have you done as I asked?'

It takes Annabel a moment to realise he's fired a question at her. 'What?' She frowns, before noticing the dangerous look in his eyes. The shiver that runs over her skin is surely just a reaction to the subterranean chill. The air itself down here seems thin, making it difficult for her to draw a decent breath.

'Don't play with me, Annabel. Are you wearing stockings and nothing else under that skirt, like I asked?'

The bottles on the tray tinkle as she gasps in outrage. 'Of course I'm not!'

'Of course you're not,' he confirms with a particular relish that starts alarm bells ringing in her head. She watches as he slips his hand into the pocket of his trousers and draws out a black-handled waiter's friend. 'You should know that defiance only makes me more determined,' he says, flipping the serrated foil cutter out from the recessed slot at one end.

'What – what do you think you're doing?'

The bottles rattle in earnest.

'Only what you should have done.' He begins circling around her.

'I never said I'd do anything,' she bursts out, trying to keep the tray steady as the bottles clink and clank. 'I'm not some sex toy for you to play your sleazy games with.'

Panic hits when she can no longer see him. 'If you dare touch me I'll scream!'

'I agree,' he says over her shoulder. 'When I do get around to touching you, you *will* scream. Loudly and repeatedly. But I promise you that won't be tonight. Or tomorrow. Or even next week. No matter how much you beg for it, Annabel, I won't touch you until you're properly ready for me.'

'What the hell are you doing right now, then?' she demands, referring to a tug she feels on the hem of her skirt. 'Stop it!' she shouts as she feels it rise up her thighs. 'I don't want this.'

And just like that he's gone. 'No one's keeping you here against your will. You're free to go any time you want. Just take the tray and walk up those stairs and I'll never bother you again.'

He's right, Annabel realises, with shock. Why is she standing here taking this like she doesn't have a choice? The bottles on the tray have set up an almost constant chiming by now, as her arms tremble with the effort of holding the tray aloft. Go! she urges herself, but can't seem to make her feet move to obey. Much as it shames her to admit it, there's a part of her that responds to him, that wants this. With a strange little noise of defeat, she stays where she is and closes her eyes.

'Good girl.' She hears approval in her ear and feels the pull on her skirt again. 'Just let it all go and do as I say.'

True to his word, his fingers never so much as brush her skin as he raises her skirt up over her hips, even though she's desperate for him to touch her now that he's said he won't.

He steps back around in front of her and sweeps his gaze over her from head to foot. 'Tights, Annabel?' He gives her a look that says she'll be sorry and drops into a crouch.

She shifts the tray to try to see what he's doing, but gives up when the movement sets some of the bottles wobbling precariously.

'Careful now, you need to keep nice and still,' he warns, and she feels her tights being stretched away from her skin, followed by the tugging shred and tear as he takes to the gusset with the foil cutter. 'In future, if I tell you to do something, you do it without question, without hesitation.'

Annabel gasps as the cool air hits her heated flesh. She feels one side of her knickers being pulled away from her hip.

'I told you I wanted to see what treasures you're hiding down here,' he says, slicing through the narrow band of fabric, then moving to do the same on the other side before pulling the ruined garment free.

Annabel's breath sticks in her throat. The sudden stillness and silence of the cellar become charged while she shivers and blushes under the most intimate scrutiny of her life.

'I knew you were a natural redhead, Annabel,' Aidan says at last, his soft accent roughened around the edges. 'And you smell divine. Cinnamon and spice – what a combination.' He pushes back to his feet and her belly clenches to see him holding her knickers to his nose. 'I look forward to getting my tongue in there and lapping you up.'

He reaches out and levels the drooping front edge of the tray with a finger, stopping the bottles from sliding to the floor. The twitch and burn of her locked muscles and the dizzying pounding of her blood are so acute Annabel fears she can't hold on much longer.

'Think how good it will feel to have me licking you all over until you're dripping wet, how satisfying it will be to have my fingers buried inside that slick little cunt. I'll only use two to start with, so I can push them deep and explore every inch, hunting out all your weak spots. Then, when I've got to know you better than you know yourself, I'll stretch you with a third and finger-fuck you, hard.'

'Please.' Annabel's voice is breathy and desperate as the bottles shake along with her entire body. 'I'm going to drop the tray.'

Aidan just smiles at her, those blue eyes blazing into hers. 'But, because you've displeased me, I won't let you come, Annabel. Not for a long, long time. Instead, I'll use all that newfound knowledge to drive you to the edge and keep you there until you cry and beg and fight for release. And when you think you can't take any more, think that surely I must grant you mercy, I'm going to tie you down and take my own pleasure in every way imaginable, until I'm the only thing you can taste and smell and feel. I'm going to claim ownership of all of you, from those plump ruby lips to the hot-pink glow of your spanked arse, and you're going to surrender willingly and love every minute of it.'

Mouth dry, heart hammering, she nearly faints with need when he reaches for her. Rather than touch the throbbing ache between her legs as she silently begs him to do, he pulls her skirt back down into place and checks his wristwatch.

'Time for another busy night, Ms Frost. I'm going to enjoy watching you work knowing you're secretly exposed and wet for me.' He takes the tray from her and heads for the stairs. 'Remember that, every time you catch me looking. Tomorrow, I'll want you to tell me how it made you feel.'

His for a Day
Penny Birch

Morris Rathwell smiled, a greasy, knowing smirk. 'Looks like it's time for forfeits, Penny,' he said, making no effort to conceal his pleasure at the thought of watching me spanked, piddled on or worse.

'Not necessarily,' I answered, fingering my cards as I wondered how I could get out of the hole I'd dug for myself.

The game had started well. I'd had Melody stripped down to her knickers before I'd even had to take my top off, while Morris himself had had such a bad run of cards he'd barely participated. Harmony had been luckier, catching me out in a bluff to get me down to my panties and bra, but she was in the same embarrassing condition herself. The last player, Edmund Knowles, hadn't done

72

too well either, and was sitting in nothing but a pair of pink boxer shorts decorated with hearts, which served to confirm my opinion of his sexuality.

Now I was in trouble. I was already obliged to go nude if I lost, but, while Morris and Melody had dropped out and I was sure Harmony was bluffing again, I needed to be able to offer something to stay in the game. At the very least she was going to want a chance to spank me, but I was determined that, just for once in my life, I was not going to end up with my bare bottom getting tanned in front of an audience. Not that I minded a good spanking so much, but there was always something peculiarly humiliating about being done in front of Morris and his wife, besides having to suffer Edmund Knowles' camp witticisms at my expense.

'Come along, Penny,' Morris urged. 'What's it to be?'

'I'll be slave for a day,' I offered, 'but I need to see you both, and, if I win, then whoever has the worst hand is mine, on the same terms.'

Edmund appeared to have found a loose thread on his boxers and didn't respond at all, but then I was fairly sure he had a mediocre hand, certainly nothing to match my full house of aces over fives. Besides, he was obviously gay and so would probably make me spend my Sunday tidying his house. He was good company too, with a sharp sense of humour I couldn't help but enjoy, at least as long as it wasn't directed at me while I was having my bare bottom smacked. If Harmony wasn't bluffing, then my fate would be tougher, a day of hardcore lesbian sex with me very firmly on the receiving end, but even then I would have the pleasure of denying Morris and Melody their share, or so I assumed.

'What do you mean by slave?' Harmony asked. 'Obviously I can't sell you, or brand you, or have "Slut Hole" tattooed on your cunt, more's the pity, but can I give you to Morris to fuck, or make you lick Mel?'

Her manner was exactly as it had been when she'd bluffed before, but I wasn't having it and decided to risk a further surrender of my dignity. Besides, whatever they did to me, I knew I'd enjoy it in the end.

'You can do as you like with me,' I told her, 'as long as it's safe, sane and consensual, of course, so no permanent marks, but, yes, you can lend me to other people if you want to.'

I'd got her. If she was bluffing, she'd have to decline my offer, which would give her away and she'd have to strip while I kept my underwear. Otherwise she had to show her cards and hope that she could beat me, which was unlikely.

'I accept,' she answered. 'Edmund?'

He looked up, glancing first at her, then at me. 'Eh? Oh, yes, darlings, that's just fine.'

I wondered what I'd do with him if he turned out to have the losing hand. He was attractive, well built and very well groomed, and from what little I knew of his reputation he'd play fair and take his role seriously. Harmony, on the other hand, was going to suffer. I'd start by caning her in front of Morris and Melody, then take her to bed for sex, only to make her sleep on the floor once I'd had my fun. I owed her that and more, adding the prospect of sweet revenge to my increasing arousal. That assumed she lost, as her hand evidently wasn't as useless as I'd supposed.

'Come on then, Harmony,' I urged. 'Let's see you.'

She began to lay her cards down, one at a time, a three, another three, a third, and my stomach went tight at the thought of her having four of a kind. The next card was a king, the last a four and I was grinning with triumph and relief.

'Full house,' I announced, laying down my own cards, 'aces over fives, and you are in big trouble, Miss Harmony.'

'What about Edmund?' she answered me.

'I have an orgy,' he announced, 'and just the sort I like best, a queen and four jacks.'

* * *

I stood in the hallway of Edmund Knowles' flat, still full of the bitter chagrin I'd been suffering ever since he won me as his slave for the day, and feeling very silly indeed.

It had been all right at first, when he'd allowed me to start my twenty-four hours the following morning instead of giving me to the others to play with, but since waking up I'd discovered that his motives were purely selfish. I'd also discovered that, however much he might like men, he was not purely gay.

We'd slept together at his flat, and when we'd gone to bed he'd shown no interest in me beyond commenting on how large and soft my bottom felt in his lap as he cuddled up to me. I'd got a surprisingly good night's sleep, only to be woken by the feel of his hand in my hair as he guided me down under the duvet and on to his morning erection. It was a shock, at first, but a bet's a bet and it was hardly the first time I'd taken a man's cock in my mouth, but as I sucked I was thinking of how things should have been, with my thighs spread to Harmony as she buried her pretty face in my pussy.

Once he'd done his business in my mouth, and insisted I swallow, he'd got me out of bed with a slap to my bottom and demanded coffee and toast. I'd done it nude, hoping to please him, but he'd complained the coffee was too hot and made me kneel for a spanking with his slipper, leaving me with a red bottom and feeling even more sorry for myself. I'd then been given a pinny and told to get on with the housework, tidying his flat with my body nude but for the frilly apron that barely covered my breasts and left my rear view not merely exposed but set off by the bow tied in the small of my back.

He'd gone shopping, leaving me with instructions to have the kitchen and loo immaculate by the time he got back. I'd done my best, scrubbing and polishing on my hands and knees, but I'd been far from finished when he returned. My punishment had been another spanking, this time administered with a big wooden bath brush as I bent over the lavatory bowl. He'd then announced that he had guests coming for Sunday lunch and that I was to cook and serve, still naked but for my pinny and with my very obviously smacked bottom on show behind, which was how I was as I stood by his front door with a tray of hors d'oeuvres in my hands.

I had no idea who the guests were, although it seemed safe to assume that it wasn't going to be the local vicar and his wife, at least not unless they enjoyed being served by near-naked women. All I knew about Edmund was that he'd met Melody Rathwell at a burlesque club on a night that featured male strippers, and that she'd been sufficiently impressed to invite him to the party that had ended with our game of strip poker. He'd told me very little since, being more interested in enjoying his control over me.

The buzzer went and my heart seemed to skip a beat, but I did as I'd been ordered and answered it, then pulled the latch back on the door and stood to attention with my tray. I heard footsteps on the stairs, and voices, all male, to my relief. While I knew I could cope with men, and especially gay men, having to serve another woman would be far more humiliating. I was also hoping that Edmund would come out and explain the situation, sparing me the shame of being found as I was and inspected by his guests. He stayed where he was in the living room and my face was hot with blushes as the door swung open to admit three men, all dressed in smart but casual clothes and all stopping in astonishment as they saw me. I curtsied as best I could, determined to play my part well and hopefully avoid another spanking, although I was fairly sure I was going to get it anyway, and in front of everybody.

'Hors d'oeuvres, sirs?' I offered.

The first of them, a tall man with floppy blond hair and a blue roll-neck jumper, accepted an hors d'oeuvre then moved to the side, peering at me in amazement and lifting his eyebrows as he saw I was bare behind.

'Well, I never,' he remarked as his friends crowded in behind him. 'I do like your new maid, Edmund, but I'd have thought, a boy, perhaps? You know, some muscular young Apollo in need of a few quid a week and not wholly impartial to cock.'

The others made noises of agreement, addressed to Edmund, who'd appeared in the living-room doorway a moment too late to make the introductions and spare at least some of my blushes. He came close, adjusted my pinny so that my nipples were barely covered, applied a firm slap to my bottom and then turned to his guests, greeting each with a kiss before he bothered to explain what was going on.

'This is Penny,' he said. 'I won her in a game of cards last night. Penny, say hello to Mitchel, and Simon, and Henry.'

I smiled and bobbed another curtsy as he went on.

'She's mine to do with as I please, and, of course, as my guests, that goes for you too. Obviously she's a girl and comes complete with boobies and a big wobbly bottom and all that sort of thing, but she does give good head.'

'I bet she does,' the one called Simon remarked as he moved round behind me to inspect my back and bottom.

He was small, only a little taller than me, and wiry, with a delicate, almost elfin, face and a naturally mocking expression. The third man, Henry, was tall and fat and seemed to have modelled himself on Oscar Wilde. I stood stock still as they inspected me, determined not to give Edmund an excuse to dish out another punishment. The buzzer went for a second time and I put my tray down to answer it, being careful to bend from the waist, which drew a comment from Mitchel.

'She's like a little bunny girl, how sweet! Who else have you invited, Edmund?'

'Just Jack and his new twink.'

'Jack has a new twink?'

'Jack does have a new twink, and I for one am green with envy. Put it this way, if you want your muscular young Apollo you could do a lot worse. It's fresh out of public school and deliciously naïve, as green as a cucumber, I swear.'

'Does Jack lend it out?'

'Oh, you know what Jack's like. What he can do to you, you can do to his twink, so it's really just a question of whether you think you can accommodate him. Hush, here he comes.'

The laughter that had greeted Edmund's remarks died at the sound of a heavy tread on the stairs. I got into position, standing to attention with my tray of hors d'oeuvres held out, but when the door swung open I nearly dropped the lot. The man who'd come in was obviously Jack, and he was huge, well over six feet tall, with massive shoulders made more bulky still by a padded, knee-length leather coat, with a thick waist and solid hips. He gave me a puzzled look, not unfriendly but somehow aggressive, and I found my voice cracking as I offered him the plate.

A hand like a spade reached out to scoop up half of the remaining hors d'oeuvres before he cocked a thumb at me. 'What's this?'

'My maid,' Edmund explained. 'I won her at cards. Do

80

come in. And this must be golden boy himself? Adrian, isn't it?'

It was only as Jack stepped aside that I realised his boyfriend had been standing behind him. Adrian was everything Edmund had described, tall, lean and obviously well muscled, but with a mop of blond curls and an almost feminine delicacy to his face that made him seem soft. He was also openly nervous, his eyes flicking to my half-exposed chest as he took an hors d'oeuvre, and his cheeks immediately flushing pink.

'Look all you like,' Edmund offered, 'and don't hesitate to touch. She's here for our amusement.'

'You keep your hands to yourself,' Jack warned, making the others laugh, although they all sounded more than a little nervous.

Adrian had gone bright pink and opened his mouth to speak, only to think better of it.

'Do come through,' Edmund offered, speaking quickly in an effort to defuse the situation. 'Penny, you had better get on with the vegetables.'

I waited until all six of them were through the door, then hurried to the kitchen. The door was open and I could hear them talking in the living room, Edmund playing the polite host but Jack dominating the conversation as he dominated everything around him. I got to work, wondering if they'd be content with using me as a serving girl, or if I'd find myself obliged to surrender myself to something more intimate. Edmund had already proved that he didn't mind girls, while the look in Adrian's eyes had been unmistakable. Mitchel, Simon and Henry seemed to be purely gay, but Jack looked super-masculine, the sort who'd be equally happy with male or female as long as they were prepared to surrender to him. I wanted to as well, at a purely chemical level, but I couldn't help but react against his overbearing personality.

Lunch went smoothly. I'd been doing Sunday roasts since I was a little girl, while to judge by what was in the kitchen Edmund did his cooking from a recipe book. They were easy to impress, and full of praise for my ability, Edmund picking fault only once, in order to give himself an excuse to spank me, this time over his knee, with the others laughing as my bottom was turned pink once more.

By the time I'd put out a bowl of fruit on the living-room table and served them whisky, they were joking that it was a pity Edmund didn't really own me. Jack was spread out in the most comfortable armchair, his feet up on Adrian's back, completely at ease and so much the dominant personality in the room that he brought to mind a silverback gorilla with his troop.

'Have you fucked her?' he asked Edmund.

'Not really my thing,' Edmund answered, 'although I did make her suck me off this morning, and she is good. Take her into the bedroom, if you'd like to try her out?'

I froze to the spot, my stomach tight, my throat blocked by a lump that seemed to be the size of a golf ball. Jack stirred lazily in his chair, his hard gaze moving from my feet to my head and back. Then he spoke. 'Yeah, why not?'

He got up, towering over me as he took my arm in a grip I knew I couldn't possibly break, to march me into the bedroom without bothering to look back. I heard the others laughing as I was thrown down on the bed and my pinny ripped off to leave me nude and vulnerable, my thighs already open to him, unable to resist his sheer masculinity for all my misgivings. He was pulling down his zip as he climbed on to the bed, only not between my legs but close to my head.

'Suck me hard.'

His cock was already in my mouth and I was already sucking, with one hand toying with his massive balls and the other between my legs. I was scared I wouldn't be wet enough to take him, but I needn't have worried, my pussy already juicing so freely I'd have been able to take a man twice his size. Still I began to tease my clit, only to have my hand snatched away and replaced with his, larger by far, and rougher, kneading my sex as if I were a lump of dough. It hurt, but that didn't stop me squirming against his hand. He laughed to find me so eager and put his free hand to his cock, masturbating into my mouth as I sucked.

83

'What a willing little slut you are!' he joked. 'Still, that's Big Jack for you, the best in the business. I've had men who've never so much as wanked a friend bend over and beg for it up the arse, I have, and more little tarts like you than you've had hot dinners.'

My efforts at cock sucking were having results, either that or he was getting turned on by the sound of his own voice, as his cock was already hard, the meaty foreskin peeled right back to leave me working on a fat, glossy knob as he tugged himself into my mouth. I'd have happily finished him like that, but he had other ideas, pulling back to mount me, simply by twisting me around so that my pussy was where my mouth had been and stuffing his cock in to the hilt. The sheer force of it made me cry out, and he quickly rolled me up and grabbed hold of my thighs, looking down at my helpless body as he fucked me. It was so hard and so fast I could do nothing but lie back, gasping out my feelings as my body jerked and shivered to his thrusts.

I tried to hold back from putting a hand between my legs and bringing myself off as he fucked me, knowing it would signal my complete surrender, but just as my will broke he gave a hard grunt, jammed himself deep and stopped, holding himself so far up me that his balls were squashed between my well-spread bottom cheeks as he emptied their contents into my body. My hand was already on my pussy, but for no very obvious reason he seemed to think I'd already come.

He spoke as he pulled out. 'You've never had it like that, have you? Maybe you never will again.'

He stood up and moved away to wipe his cock on my ruined pinny. I didn't answer, dizzy from my reaction to my sudden rough fucking, but far from finished. He left, without even closing the door, so that the others had a clear view of me lying fucked and sweaty on the bed, with my thighs still apart, struggling against my need to disgrace myself completely by masturbating in front of them.

Jack made another of his remarks and the rest of them laughed, as usual, before Adrian spoke up. 'May I, please, Jack? I've never done it with a woman.'

Jack just laughed. 'OK, just so you learn that there is nothing, but nothing half so good as being with Big Jack.'

I lay back, already resigned to my fate, for all my instinctive resentment at being given away so casually, and not even by Edmund, who had won the right, but by Jack, who simply assumed that he was boss. Not that I minded Adrian, who was not only beautiful but rather sweet. When he came in I greeted him with a smile, then gestured to the door, which he shut, and locked. He was obviously nervous, but the bulge in his trousers suggested he was excited too, while I urgently needed somebody who would show me a bit more consideration than Jack. I opened my arms as Adrian approached the bed.

He came to me, hesitant, clearly not happy to do anything unless I wanted it, which ensured that he got what he wanted, and more. I took him in my arms, kissed him and felt him respond. I took one hand and put it to my chest, allowing him to feel my breasts as I unzipped his trousers and pulled out his cock. He was lovely, big and smooth, and very hard, a delight to hold in my hand and a delight to suck. I kissed his balls and teased his bottom hole, let him explore mine and lick my pussy, which he was desperate to do.

When he first entered me he was on top, but I let him have me every way he wanted, with me riding his body one way and then the other, on my side with my bottom stuck out into his lap, face-down with him mounted on my back and finally doggy, with me on all fours as he pumped into me and I masturbated in open, shameless delight for the feel of his cock inside me and the rude position I was in.

I came first, a lovely long orgasm that made me cry out in pure ecstasy, a reaction I was hoping Jack had heard and understood even as I came down from my peak. Adrian had obviously been holding back for me, that or having me come on his erection was too much for him, because I'd barely stopped moaning when he whipped his cock free to spunk up all over my bottom, apologising for the mess he was making even as he milked himself over my cheeks and into my slit. He even fetched tissues and mopped me up before collapsing next to me on the bed, grinning sheepishly.

I kissed his cheek. 'That was good, better than Jack.'

'Nobody is better than Jack.'

'*You* are, at least with girls. Was that really your first time?'

'Yes, and it was good, so good. You're so lovely, Penny, so soft, so ... so cuddly. I think I'm in love with you!'

'Don't be silly. We've only just met. Besides, you're Jack's boyfriend, and presumably gay, well ... sort of.'

'I'm not gay! I'm bisexual, I suppose, but I've never had a chance, and with Jack ...'

To my astonishment he began to cry. I cuddled up to him, stroking his hair as he poured out his feelings to me, about how he loved Jack but he was desperate to escape the constant control, and to be free to lead his own life. In the end I got up and went to pull on my clothes, which were still on Edmund's bedside chair. There was a fire escape outside the window and I had every intention of using it, but when I beckoned to Adrian he hesitated.

'But what about Jack? And what about you? I thought you belonged to Edmund for the day?'

'Never mind Jack, or Edmund. One thing you have to learn, Adrian, is that nobody belongs to anybody else, not unless they want to, whether it's just for one day or for ever.'

Deeper Access
Valerie Grey

My first time in a lesbian bar: I am finally legal, just two days past my twenty-first birthday, out with all the grown-up dykes.

Or so my fake ID states.

I'm really not, but I look old enough, and nineteen is not far off.

I've been told they don't really care at this lesbian bar; that older women often come here looking for young girls to have fun with.

And *that's* what I want.

Already I feel self-conscious, the girl who doesn't belong here, doesn't know what she's in for.

It's pretty much empty, just past seven o'clock. I have my choice of spots and I choose a barstool at the curved end of the bar, where I can see as much as possible.

I'm the only one there, and the bartender is friendly, calls me 'Sweetie'. I try to be cool as I order a glass of sauvignon blanc.

'First time here?' she asks. 'Well, just relax, hon, and have a good time. Everybody's pretty nice here; they'll treat you good. Especially you: you're cute.'

She touches me lightly under the chin, and I give her a smile in return.

I wonder if she's coming on to me, the friendly flirty bartender.

The dance floor is empty, but I notice there are darker spots around the perimeter that are more populated: two women together in several spots, a larger group in one area, and a number of single women at tables.

I wonder if the single women are waiting for friends or if they are there, like me, to find new ones. I try to subtly check them out, but it's too hard to tell from this distance.

I sip my wine for a while, hoping that the drink works its magic on my nerves without getting too out of hand. In about thirty minutes, I finish the first glass and order another. The warm glow of the alcohol is starting, and I feel myself more relaxed.

The barstools have started to fill up; I can blend into the background more.

It's a diverse group: a few butch girls, some 'soft', some harder, some femme types like me, and even a couple of 'bull-dykes'. I notice the latter two eyeing me and I start to get uneasy; not my type, for sure. But when I avoid their stares and show no interest, they get the hint and go back to their conversation.

My second glass of wine arrives and someone new sits down at the other end of the bar. I have a clear view of her. She's the type of woman that always draws my attention: attractive and feminine, not a lipstick, but well dressed, professional-looking, the kind of lady who is the boss. Her long hair looks to be a darker brown than my own, or maybe black, but as she moves into the light I see that it's actually a deep red. It falls over her shoulders, about the same length as my own, and frames a face of ice-cool beauty.

My guess is she's in her late thirties. She carries herself in a way that exudes strength, confidence and competence. She's clearly in charge of others out in the professional world, where she has just come from, seeking another world where girls seek her.

I drink my wine and continue to survey the room, but my gaze keeps returning to this mystery woman; she is doing her own survey, like a lioness stalking prey. As I glance back one more time, I'm surprised to see her looking *directly* at me.

I try to smile, but I just can't, I'm too nervous, and

then it's over and she's off to someone else. I exhale and realise that I had stopped breathing during our visual encounter.

I gulp the rest of my wine and want to order another, but I know I should slow down. I wait. I distract myself for a while by reading the signs behind the bar and watching the bartender fill drink orders.

She is looking at me again; the stare is longer, more intense, like she's considering the possibilities I present. Her mouth forms an almost-smile; it's not one of affection or friendliness. It's more like she's smiling to herself, like she's figured me out. She is an experienced woman, I know; and she has known many inexperienced girls like me.

I order a third drink, keeping my eyes down, waiting for it, and it comes: a low, silky voice in my left ear: 'Why don't you let me get that.'

Here she is: her face inches from mine. I try to stay cool as I accept her offer. I start to ask her to sit, but she doesn't need an invitation and takes the seat next to me without asking.

'I'm Hannah,' she says, running a long insistent finger down the inside of my thigh.

She's confident. I wish I were that sure of myself.

She leans back on the stool, facing me. The smile is more obvious this time, but still formal and controlled. Her eyes continue to lock on to mine, still probing, analysing me.

'A newbie. I thought you looked young. You *are* young.'

I tell her my name is Jolene. I worry that she may dismiss me as *too* young, but in fact this seems to entice her.

We chat for a while and I become a little more comfortable with her, though she still maintains a distance between us, and it's clear that she is a cut above me. From the conversation, I surmise that she is in her early thirties, and I can tell that she is extremely intelligent. It turns out my guess was right: she is a professional, a lawyer, and, judging by her clothes, a pretty successful one.

She's wearing a slinky, expensive-looking skirt, subdued but well-crafted jewellery and a beautiful silk top, whose plunging neckline provides a lovely view of her creamy cleavage. She just exudes class and power.

'So,' she says, 'should I *go easy* on you?'

Her lips move easily into a smirk. She seems to sense that I'm really ready for her.

'No,' I say, trying to sound annoyed and confident. 'I may be young, but I'm not *innocent*.'

That draws an outright laugh from Hannah and the only genuine smile I've seen so far.

'So you're not innocent?' There is a gentle mocking tone in her voice. 'OK, OK, I *like* that. Out in the big world and ready for adventure. My kind of girl.'

She offers her glass as in a toast, and I smile sheepishly, but feel good that she smiled and still seems interested.

As I'm trying to think of something else to say, Hannah startles me. She leans in close and looks me intently in the eyes for several long seconds. Finally, she whispers, so only I can hear her: 'You're sub, aren't you?'

I am astonished by her insight. She leans back and gives me that same intense, icy gaze, like an anthropologist would give to a feral bitch in heat.

'Yeah, I can always tell, spot it a mile away.'

I open my mouth ... and nothing.

She takes a sip of her drink and continues, 'Something about the eyes, there's a "yearning", a need. And you've definitely got it, girl. You may not even know it.'

My silence acknowledges the truth in her words.

Her pretty mouth transforms into a leer. 'It's all good,' she says, 'I enjoy subs, *a lot*.' Her voice is filled with both promise and warning.

Hannah suggests that we move to someplace more private and points to one of the booths in the dark regions of the bar. Thrilled at the way things are going, I nod.

In the booth, Hannah places a hand on my thigh and urges me closer so we can 'get to know each other'. I slide over and my leg is against her, finding the warmth of her thigh just as intoxicating as the drinks I've been having. She runs her fingers boldly up and down my leg as she studies my face for a reaction. I move my legs farther apart as her hand reaches the spot between them.

She rubs me through my jeans and says, 'Not so innocent, indeed.'

As if to prove the point, she takes my left hand in hers and places it in her lap. Her eyes stay locked on to mine as she then slips it under her skirt and up into her crotch. My heart beats faster as I feel the silky fabric of her panties and the obvious warmth beneath it.

'Go ahead, little one,' she says, 'explore.'

I let my fingers wander over the fabric until I find the edge and slip inside. I feel a small tuft of hair and then find the moist cleft at her centre. My trembling fingers slip inside to find the warm liquid of her cunt. Her response is pleasant and reserved, a barely perceptible gasp under her breath. She spreads her legs just a bit for me and leans back as I spend the next several minutes playing inside her. The feel of her heat around my fingers and the whole situation have me extremely excited. Hannah seems completely calm and detached, but I'm pretty sure this is just a matter of self-control.

'Does it feel good in there? You really like having your fingers in me, don't you?'

Her eyes move back and forth, studying my reaction; a look of recognition is on her worldly face. 'You're dying to lick me, too, aren't you? The idea that I might

94

let you get your face between my legs is just driving you wild. Oh, I *do love* subbies.'

She moves in, her face inches from mine, and she chuckles as she feels my fingers acting more intently. 'You can almost *taste* it, can't you? Don't deny it; we both know it's true.'

She pulls my hand from between her legs and urges it firmly towards my mouth. 'Go ahead, girl, *indulge*.'

I place the wet fingers in my mouth and close my eyes as I get my first tawdry taste of her essence. I lick them clean and wonder if anyone is watching this little exhibition. Behind the bar, I see the bartender taking it all in, nodding her head with approval.

'You taste tasty,' I say.

She grips my hair, pulls my head back, kisses me, her red lipstick lips gliding over my trembling clear lips; her tongue dips lightly into my mouth, like a doe at a pond, sliding along my teeth.

I feel the moisture in my panties.

She gets aggressive, oblivious to anyone else in the room. Her mouth devours mine as her hands wander over me like I'm her personal possession. Her left hand reaches boldly up my top while her right goes down the back of my pants. I feel her fingers exploring between my butt cheeks until one finds my asshole, firmly circles it, and then nudges the tip inside. I moan shamelessly against her tongue. I love ass play, but this is more than that: it's a show of power, an invasion of my most private spot, in a public place, an indication that she can and will do whatever she wants to me.

'You little *slut*,' she whispers, 'you *like* my finger up your butt, don't you?'

I respond with open eyes.

'Well, I like it, too,' she breathes, her fingertip inching deeper into me. 'And, when we're done tonight, I'll enjoy knowing I've had my fingers way up inside your sweet little bottom, and I'll remember how you squirmed and begged for more.'

She is driving me bughouse, stimulating both my body and my mind. At that moment, I just need to go somewhere with her and do anything and everything she wants.

She kisses me again and I sense her passion growing like mine, and then she breaks it off.

'You know what?' she says. She has that same commanding look in her eyes as she continues, quite matter-of-factly, 'I think it's time you *sucked* me. Get under the table.'

I'm shocked and I hesitate, looking around us. She wants me – no, *expects* me to lick her right here, now, with all these people around. Unable to resist, I look quickly around the room to see if anyone is watching, then slip down into the darkness.

My face is just inches from the crotch of her panties. A heady aroma fills my nostrils. I place my mouth directly over her panty-covered mound and suck gently on the fabric, taking in the soft flesh beneath it.

I suck; my tongue works up and down over the hidden slit, and I feel the first fluids seeping out of her. Her hips edge forward just a bit and I can tell she likes what I'm doing for her. I'm really excited now. My one hand moves to caress her thigh while the other pulls her panty aside, providing direct access to the delicate flesh of her pussy. I place a gentle kiss on her wetness, then a quick, soft lick. I'm about to dig deeper into her sweetness when suddenly it's over, just as quickly as it began.

Her hand is in my hair again, and I groan in frustration as she pulls me away.

'Get back up here,' she says.

There's a satisfied smirk on her face as I shimmy back up into the booth. It's clear to me now that this was a test, not of my sexual ability, but of my willingness to please her.

'Sorry, little girl,' she says. 'I know you enjoyed doing that, but I just needed to see if you're worth my time.'

I search her face for a clue, hoping the answer is yes.

She runs her finger lightly over my lower lip.

'Don't worry,' she says. 'You passed. That's a talented little mouth you have there, girl. I'm going to enjoy you.'

The way she says 'enjoy you' makes me wetter than ever.

When I came here tonight I didn't know what I was

looking for, but I know now. I want badly to experience what this woman has to offer.

We sit and drink a while and continue the conversation, which now turns more seriously to the situation at hand.

'You know,' she says, 'I don't usually go for ones as young as you.'

I don't know why she thinks this, but I'm not going to argue.

'Of course,' she says, 'sometimes you younger ones can't handle my tastes. I've had a couple of bad experiences, misunderstandings.'

I look at her inquisitively, hoping for more explanation.

'The fact is,' she says, 'a younger woman can be very exciting for me, but I can be a really nasty bitch. And I don't just mean saying nasty *things*. Sometimes a young woman can be a really *naughty girl*, and must be taught a lesson. In fact, I very much enjoy teaching them a lesson, but sometimes they're not ready for it, can't handle it.' She looks directly at me now, very intent on making her point clear. 'Do you understand, little girl?'

If the point wasn't clear before, the tone of 'little girl' makes it abundantly so. I nod my understanding, muttering a low 'uh huh' to go with it. I've never played the sort of games she's talking about, but I've thought about it, and looking at her now, and having experienced pleasures with her so far this evening, she definitely has my attention.

For the time being, Hannah seems satisfied with my answer. We continue drinking, more or less in silence, watching the crowd of women who are starting to fill the dance floor, some of them staring at us. She takes the opportunity to kiss me. We mesh together, and her kisses become more ardent as my fingers get busy between her legs. This time I have a better chance to 'explore' and I take full advantage. Her pussy is hot and slick, her outer lips plump, and I can feel the firm bump of her already erect clitoris.

I'm pressed against her full breasts, and I can feel her nipples poking through the fabric of her thin bra and blouse. I'm amazed at her composure, despite her obvious physical arousal. The change in her breathing is barely noticeable, and the only sign of response to my manipulations is an occasional flex of her thighs around my hand. Still, her kissing is clearly inspired and, for my part, I am quickly spinning out of control.

She breaks our kiss and says, 'So, little Jolene, are you ready to go home with me?'

I'm so excited now that I can only nod my acceptance, but Hannah wants more assurance. 'Are you sure you can handle this? Everything? Remember what I said: I can be a nasty bitch when I want to.'

I think about what she's said, about 'naughty girls' and 'lessons' and situations I've never been in before. Part of me is scared, but a bigger part is so, so ready to go with her – more ready because her hand is back between my legs, firmly massaging my clit through the thick denim of my jeans.

I manage to push a single, desperate word from my lips: '*Please*.'

We get up to leave. Hannah's arm is around my waist, and it's clear that she is showing me off, proud to show everyone her conquest for tonight. Her hand is on my rear, gently squeezing my buns as we walk.

'You have a *sweet* little butt, girl,' she tells me. 'I'm going to have so much *fun* with you.'

I'm excited by her comment, and scared.

We walk quickly to a nearby garage where Hannah's car is parked. Not surprisingly, it's a nice one: a Mercedes convertible, a two-seater that looks brand new. Hannah opens the passenger door for me and I climb into the nicest car I've ever ridden in.

Hannah drives. I look down at her lap and think about how I diddled her back in the bar. These thoughts keep me excited as we drive along the water. We head towards a series of high-rises and ultimately turn into the garage attached to one of them.

We hop on the elevator and stand in 'elevator silence' as it rises to one of the upper floors. I'm dying to touch her again, but she shows no interest at the moment, so I restrain myself.

From the elevator it's a brief walk down the hall to Hannah's condo. She unlocks the door and lets me in.

Her place is amazing: large and exquisitely furnished. I start to comment on it, but, before I can, Hannah is on me, pinning me against the door, her hands cupping my rear as she lifts me slightly to adjust for our heights.

She seems different from the bar. She kisses me, her mouth open and wanton, her tongue plunging into my mouth like a skydiver, where it is met with my own daredevil tongue.

Now her hands are more active, cupping my breasts through my shirt and bra, then quickly moving down to tug at my belt. I help her undo it and then she's at my pants, opening the button and zipper and pushing the jeans down over my hips.

My top pushed up, bra unclasped, I feel the cool air hit my naked breasts. Hannah breaks our kiss for a moment to look at them. She rolls both of my nipples between her fingers, making them even harder than they already are.

'You have nice little titties, Jolene,' she says.

My whole body moves against her, begging for more sensation, but she's on her own schedule, not mine. I'm there for her enjoyment, my clothing pushed up and down to give her access to the most intimate parts of my body. It feels so good and dirty to be exposed that way, more so than being completely naked. These are the only parts of me she's really interested in, and that makes the whole situation even hotter.

Hannah bends down to take my right nipple in her mouth. She sucks, her tongue soft and wet over the sensitive flesh, gently between her teeth before gobbling all my tit into her mouth. Once that one is entirely aroused, she gives the same treatment to the other.

Her hand is between my legs, moving lightly, barely brushing over my engorged lips, making me twitch as she expertly teases me. One finger traces circles around my you-know-what. She slips it in.

She inserts two and then three fingers completely in.

Hannah licks at my throat as she moves her fingers back and forth. Her other hand explores elsewhere, the fingers rolling up and down my butt crease, a single finger circling around my anus like a mongoose around a cobra. I feel it move forward to gather some of my wet darkness, then back to my rear. I say, 'Yes,' as it slowly pushes inside.

She moves it slowly in and out, each time a little deeper.

Her finger slides all the way up into my asshole.

She whispers in my ear, 'You *do* love my finger up your poop pipe, don't you, dirty girl? What a *filthy* little slut you are.'

She's all over me. She gobbles on my breasts, ravishing

them the way men do on the covers of romance books; her left hand between my legs, three fingers working in my pussy. Her right hand, the one with fingers up my ass, that is driving me bughouse Betty. Three hard thrusts up the ass and my back arches, I grab her shoulders and I come, come in my cunt and in my anus, an assault on the feeble membrane that separates the two.

I shake in her arms like it's a St Vitus Dance, little cries like little birds forced from my little mouth; her mouth on mine again, smothering my cries with her matronly lips as her hands continue to work me down below. I try to spread my legs more but it's hard while I'm standing. Hannah sees this and reacts, pinning me against the wall.

I raise my left leg to allow deeper access.

I feel her finger slip out of my bottom and for a second I'm distraught as she changes methodology: her thumb into my pussy as two fingers ram into my anus.

Picture in my mind: my fluids dripping off her hand. That sets me off again, whimpering like a whipped dog.

I come a second time.

A final squeeze and she slips all of her fingers out. She kisses me, my slut juices wetting my cheek.

Her own need is apparent; she wants satisfaction. Her grip on my shoulders is firm with intent and I'm being pushed down, down to my knees and to the liquid treasure that is Hannah's cunt.

She's still dressed, and she quickly undoes her skirt and drops it to the floor, revealing the black satin thong that was in my mouth earlier this evening. My hands are trembling as I reach forward and slip the flimsy thing down over her hips and thighs. Hannah steps out of it and leans forward slightly, raising her left leg and bracing her knee against the wall, to give me access to her throbbing cunt. Her lips are swollen a deep-red colour; I can glimpse the delicious pink flesh inside, already glistening with a thick coating of love juice.

This is what I've been waiting for. I can tell she's trying to maintain control. I kiss the inside of her pussy, then remove my thumbs and simply lick up and down within her slit, enjoying the silky warmth of it against the sides of my tongue.

She tries to spread her legs wider, but it's difficult in this position.

'Wait,' she says breathlessly, 'move over here.'

Hannah moves to one of the leather chairs in the room. At the same time, she slips off the rest of her clothing, and, for the first time, I see how beautiful her breasts truly are, with pale, almost translucent skin revealing several tiny blue veins on the undersides.

Hannah takes the new position, kneeling on the seat of the chair, her shoulders resting comfortably on its back.

I am to have her from behind. Her thighs lead up to

the cheeks of her ass, silky smooth, creamy white. Her pussy is framed delightfully between them, the lips pouting outward, a delicate cleft waiting for the gentle caress of an eager dirty girl's tongue.

I push my face into her, her dewy dewdrop petals entering my mouth as my nose dives deep into the crack of her ass.

She was so right about me earlier. I was dying to get my face between her legs, to please her in every way, to let my tongue roam her land of pleasure like a slut on cunt safari.

I love pussy.

I knew I'd love hers.

I'm going to do it all.

Claws
Sommer Marsden

I am not a handsome man ... He says that to me all the time. And I disagree.

He's older than me by a good ten years, taller than me by a good foot. His hair is mostly steel-grey with just a few shots and swirls of darkness in it. His nose has been broken once, twice and, if that story his brother told me once upon a time while drunk is accurate, maybe three times.

It's in the way that he carries himself that I see the beauty. The kindness tucked down there in the storm-cloud grey of his eyes. I see it in the hard jut of his chin when he's serious and the stubble on his jaw in the early morning when he goes down on me and it scratches my inner thighs.

I'm enamoured of his big strong hands that have never worked for a living at a desk but always out of doors. The laugh that rumbles out of him when he's amused – usually by me. And the way he makes me beg. The way he unfolds me like reverse origami, pulling back each intricate corner to unveil something vulnerable.

He is most beautiful when he makes me beg.

So when he points to them, in the dealer's case, looking scary all on their own, my stomach bottoms out. It gets away from me for a moment as if I am in free-fall and then I have that floaty lightheaded feeling that comes with a jolt of anxiety.

'I think we'll take those.' He's watching me with those grey eyes and ticking off each small reaction I may have. Even the ones I myself am unaware of.

Those? Those *things*? It has to be a joke. I pray it is a joke.

I shiver and there's that laugh that rumbles out of him and he puts his arm around me and pulls me in. 'We'll have fun with these, Paula,' he says, teeth pressed to my ear so I can feel the hardness of them. The potential for a painful nip or a soft kiss. You never know.

'But –'

'It's what scares us most that mesmerises us. It's why you have that irrational urge sometimes,' he says into my hair, 'to jump off the high ledge, run your finger over the edge of the kitchen knife, drive a fork into the outlet.'

I've confessed these odd fleeting thoughts to him. He's told me most folks have them, especially when stressed. It's the irrational and overwhelming urge to revolt … rebel. Even at the cost of your safety or your sanity. The siren song of a potentially deadly urge.

The vendor has a large collection on display for sale. He slips a hand inside the glass case and removes our item. They're tucked in the case, nestled against ball-gags and whips, spurs and speculums. There are crops and paddles and yet … these look the worst. The biggest, the baddest, the scariest of all.

'Put your hand out, Paula.' He presses his mouth to my hair, his hand to my back. Urging me and trapping me and soothing me all at once.

I don't like sharp things. Things that can cut and rip and slice. So, when the weight of the real leather gloves with stainless-steel tips – claws, really – hits my palm, I shiver. And I shudder. And I make a small desperate sound that makes Lawrence smile.

Lawrence, not Larry. Sometimes 'sir' if I'm begging and desperate and he's in the mood to hear me say it.

'How do they feel?' he asks, his fingers splaying wide along my waist. His hips press to my ass and I feel his hardness. Fully hard – long and ready. He could bend me over the table and …

I blink.

'Repugnant,' I whisper.

108

'Good.' To the vendor he says, 'We'll take them.'

The man nods, looking curious but bored at the same time. He takes Lawrence's money and puts the claws in a bag. They jingle wickedly.

Again that feverish kind of chill races through me and I tremble. But, under all the anticipatory terror, I'm wet.

'I think we shall take these home, clean them well and play with them.' Lawrence guides me with a firm but subtle hand at the back of my waist.

That kind of touch – what I think of as his signature touch – always makes me wet too. He is a complicated, soft-spoken, affectionate and sometimes malicious man. The blend is perfection. My love for him is overwhelming.

The ride home is slow and somewhat long and very silent. When he plays with me, it's 100 per cent. Lawrence knows my mind is spinning and spinning and dreaming up visceral images of him and me and the claws – a most terrifying threeway. And yet, I squirm in my seat to keep the pulsing slickness in my cunt at bay.

My manoeuvre fails.

'Don't move,' he says softly. And that is all he says.

I stop moving instantly. So two things happen – first, my cunt grows even more slippery and eager. Second, the need to move, the unbearable urge to *move* grows rapidly.

I chew my lip to keep from moving.

Lawrence pilots his silent luxury car into the driveway. The inside smells of leather and cinnamon air-freshener and pussy. I'm so aroused I can smell my own scent. He smiles at me to show me that he smells it too.

'We'll get there, kitten,' he says.

I almost – *almost* – move and squeeze my thighs together but catch myself at the last moment and do not.

'Good girl,' he says, leaning in to kiss me.

I feel so proud of myself and then I feel so grateful because he's pinched my nipple through my sweater and fragile cotton bra. He keeps the tender bit of flesh squeezed painfully tight while he kisses me and, when I gasp from the force of his tongue over mine, he releases me. Heat and blood and the insistent pound of my pulse flood my nipple, and my cunt offers up a sudden rush of juices.

'I don't even have to touch you to know you're wet,' he whispers and winks.

And then he is gone and I'm trying to catch my breath and my car door is flying wide. He offers me his hand and helps me out. Again his hand is possessive but tender on my lower back as he guides me down the driveway. I'm grateful for his hand because my legs feel made of gelatine.

'You'll do just fine,' he says, his lips pressed to my neck and his body pressed to mine. He's pinned me up against the front door, his erection riding the split of my ass as he reaches around me and unlocks the door.

110

Lawrence always gives me encouragement. He thinks it helps me not to panic.

I am fearful of things that cut and scratch and shred. Thus the claws. Thus the panic beating big blackbird wings in my chest. Thus his encouragement and finally … my tainted arousal.

My need and fears and faith are a tangled sticky mess. But somehow he sorts them out. Better than me, truth be told.

Here is where it would be logical for him to bind me. To tie me up and tease me with the sharpened tips that look so much like deadly talons. But no, in his mind – because he's a man who is just that clever – it is much harder to be unbound and have to keep myself still. The only things that bind me are his words and my control.

'Lie down on the bed, Paula,' he says, unbuckling his belt. 'Take everything off first, but your panties and bra.'

I chew my lip, so full of nerves I feel like I might actually levitate. Like I might leave earth and hover just above where I need to be.

I unbutton my black sweater and take off my camisole. My fingers shake and my stomach churns. Under the cami is my small white bra – demi cup with lace – and a silver necklace. My jeans don't want to part for my unsure hands and at one point he reaches over and, with one quick motion, undoes the button.

'Thank you,' I whisper and push my jeans down over my hips, thighs and calves. It's in slow motion – like a dream. I kick the jeans off along with my black flats. My panties are pink and red candy-cane stripes and say SLUT on the ass. He gave them to me for Christmas and, every time I look at them, I smile.

'Go on. Get down there.' He tucks twin hunks of my strawberry-blonde hair behind my ears and pushes me gently.

I walk to the bed with feet that feel full of concrete and sand. My body spreads out over the pale-green comforter with a sigh I don't feel coming, I only hear.

I lie so that I'm a starfish. My head between the twin stacks of pillows, hands up slightly and out, legs splayed so my toes point towards the bottom corners of the bed. It is all I can do to stay that way. It takes every shred of control I possess. For, as calm as I appear, inside of me I am chaos personified. Everything in me flurrying and scurrying with a wild panic that is accented with a gut-wrenching arousal that has my panties soaked and my cunt flexing up around nothing but what's being imagined.

'Let's see how sharp these really are,' he says. The air smells medicinal and clinical, the reek of rubbing alcohol so strong my nose tingles. He wipes each claw with a fresh cotton swab and then the gloves themselves. 'They say never to use alcohol on leather,' Lawrence informs

112

me, 'but we'll take the chance. I want them clean and sterile. I'll use some saddle soap on the hide later.'

'Huh,' he says and cocks his head at me as if we're having a conversation. 'A saddle. Something to keep in mind, right, Paula?'

He could never ride me. He'd squash me. But the image in my head of him fixing me in that leather contraption, working buckles and straps … the bite of the weight, the smell of the cowhide, it all floods my mind and I start to wriggle on the bed.

He stills me with a look.

'Yes,' I gasp. 'Something to keep in mind.'

He pulls one glove on, gets the other partly on and grunts. 'Looks like it's up to you, kid.'

I sit up when he nods and tug the second glove on to his hand. He has big hands and the gloves are a tight but perfect fit. He clinks the claws at me and smiles. 'Thank you, Little Red. Now lie down there and let the Big Bad Wolf see about cutting.'

Cutting …

The very word sets me off. Deep alarm bells sound in my gut but my body turns the tables and the beat of arousal and blood in my cunt is almost unbearable. I feel like he should be able to hear it.

I know deep down he can't hear it, but he sure as shit can see it, because he smiles at me.

'Don't move.'

113

He levers one claw, shiny and long and wicked, beneath the side of my panties. I pray that they don't cut me. I love these panties. But part of me hopes they slice right through the brightly coloured cotton like a hot knife through butter.

He tugs and the fabric stretches but doesn't break. With his free hand Lawrence holds the fabric and tugs a bit more, sawing a little. Finally, it gives but more from his strength than the sharpness, I'm fairly certain.

'Not sharp enough to cut fabric, but they are pretty intimidating. Don't you think?' he enquires softly.

His eyes sparkle and he gives me that half-smile that always turns me inside out. And then the claw, cold and clinical, is running up my inner thigh. I hold my breath and force myself to stay still, though the pounding of my heart is literally echoing through all of me.

'Good, good girl,' he says. The claw slides over the indentation of my navel, making those muscles flutter and jump. It slides a bit higher, tick-tacking along the ladder of my ribs and finally he slides the stainless steel beneath the front clasp of my bra.

My pussy delivers heat and liquid and I feel myself blush at just how much of me is turned on.

'Take this off,' he says, tugging the clasp with his prosthetic weapon.

My hands are jittering so badly I can barely take hold of the clasp and unhook it. But I finally manage and let out a relieved sigh. I don't peel back the cups, I don't expose myself, I simply put my hands back down to my sides and wait, while my cunt beats frantically and my stomach feels like I'm falling.

It's Lawrence who sits on the bed, the mattress depressing with a sigh, and pushes one cup back with the tip of his claw. Then the other. My nipples spike almost painfully hard in the cool air and he says, 'Oooh'.

The cold metal caresses one rosy nub and then the other. The sensations zinging over and under and through my skin make it almost impossible for me to stay still. But I must. So I flex my toes; it is the only thing I hope to do without drawing attention.

'Entirely still,' he says, frowning.

The claw digs into my flesh enough to deliver a dull, heated kiss of pain. Not sharp, not puncturing – just heaviness and a sense of malice. A welt appears on me like a magical symbol.

I moan and my clit throbs and my pussy clenches and I tense all of myself to keep from moving any particular part.

'Shall I drive these inside of you?'

'No.' I shake my head because I really do not want that. I've forgotten.

Lawrence is stoic and hard but he is not cruel. He knows I'd never find any pleasure in that; it's nothing more than a threat. However, he is crafty, so, when he says, 'Open your mouth,' my blood runs cold and my pussy flows hot.

I part my lips with an audible pop and he smiles at me. There is that handsome man I love. There is that man who knows me inside and out – as intimately as I know myself. Possibly more so.

The steel is cool and bitter and tastes of alcohol. I let it rest on my tongue, my eyes pinned to his.

'Suck it,' he says.

I do. I close my lips around the terrifying appendage, my head full of the smell of leather and metal. I lick along the length of the claw like it's his cock and I can feel his eyes on me. I pull my head back just a touch to lick the tip of the claw the way I lick the tip of his cock when he stuffs my mouth full of himself.

'Good.' Lawrence puts his other hand on the bulge growing in his jeans. Then he places the same hand between my legs and rubs the sheathed palm along the ridge of my sex. A burst of joy sounds through my clit, my pussy, my pelvis, and I'm too late to stifle a moan.

'Take this one off,' he says, wiggling his free hand in front of me. 'It's annoying me.'

The other clawed hand is still busy fucking my mouth. Not one but two talons are now sliding relentlessly along my tongue, impersonating that cock of his I love so much.

I work the tight leather glove off and he splays it

116

between my breasts like a small dead creature. The leather is warm on my skin, the claws cool in contrast.

He pushes three now bare fingers – a fat lot of them – deep into my cunt and fucks me there too. His claws penetrate my mouth as his fingers penetrate my pussy. I am stuffed and terrified and so fucking turned on I have to keep up the mantra in my head:

Don't move. Don't move. Do … Not … Move.

He wants me still. The test, the challenge, the *hard part* is not him teasing me with something that makes me uneasy, it's me keeping myself still and handling it.

'You're doing very well.' One of the two claws in my mouth curls against my tongue and I gag a bit. 'Do you want my cock there instead?'

I nod, my eyes flooded with tears that came with the gagging. One-handed, he takes off his jeans, then he straddles me, cock out and standing true. He paints my lips with the tip of his erection, a bit of his pre-come lubricating the sensual slide. I dart my tongue out and capture that small drop of fluid. I suck the salty tang of his skin into my mouth and he grins at me

'You have a pretty little mouth, Paula. And you know how to use it.'

I blush again, my cheeks hot. He slides into me, thrusting in earnest, and, when he reaches back behind himself and tickles my outer lips and then my clit with

117

just the tip of the claws, I almost come. A very real spasm that is almost, but not quite, hard enough to make me come wracks my cunt and I gasp around him.

'Do you want to come, pretty girl?'

I nod, my mouth still full of him, my nether lips feeling the potential kiss of cold steel. He hasn't touched me with them again, but the imaginary energy of those claws so close to me is palpable. I feel him touching me there, though he isn't. I feel the energy of his new toy mingling with mine. So I know that any moment, in a breath – in a heartbeat – he could slide one into my cunt and I would be full of those … claws.

I know they won't hurt me. They're not sharp but rather blunt. They're not wickedly tipped. They are very much for show, but the fact that they are what they are rattles me. It is an irrational fear, especially since I know that Lawrence would never hurt me for real. He plays on my fears, that's all. And he's good at it.

'Suck it,' he reminds me, tapping my forehead with one finger and sliding a claw along the top of my thigh, tracing the tender place where thigh meets hip.

I suck harder as my body gushes more of my juices at having that arched claw so close to my sex.

Lawrence finally takes my face in his hands, one of them with cool metal lengths that curve up the side of my face, over my ear and tangle in my hair. He fucks me hard with slow even strokes and I keep up with him.

I suck air through my nose and try to focus on him and not the talons resting on my scalp.

He grunts, looking tense in the face, and pulls free. 'I don't want to come that way, pretty girl. I want to come deep inside that sweet, sweet pussy.'

And he flips me over on my belly like a tiddlywink. I don't say a word, I don't make a sound, barring a simple whoosh of air that flows out of me. His gloved hand – the warm leather smelling so heady and earthy and rich – cups my breast and he pinches my nipple in a stainless-steel vice. I gasp but he robs me of even that release by hauling my hip up with his free hand and driving into me.

There is the orgasm that had escaped me – three strokes in and it's shaking me, making me tremble in his arms from a release that is born of fear and pleasure and love.

'Good girl,' he says, rocking into me, gripping me tight. 'That's a good little slut.'

I flush at the praise. When he calls me his slut, I come undone. All my words fall away. I move back to take him without thinking until he steadies me by placing his splayed hand along my lower back. One-two-three-four-five steel points dig into my flesh and I freeze.

Lawrence goes slower. I know he's dragging it out so he can lightly scrape the claws along my spine. He can feel every nuance of my cunt seizing up again, gripping him tight and making me shudder. He tickles over my back and drives into me lazily. I can imagine him back there with his eyes pinned to the place where our bodies meet. His cock sliding in and out of my rosy slit. His hips banging against my ass.

I push my head down to the mattress, arms laid under me in submission. I am inverted and powerless to him and he tickles the cold metal up and down the knobs of my spine until he sighs and says, 'So pretty. Too pretty. Good girl.'

His hands seize my hips, one muted by leather, one strong and warm. He fucks me so my long hair rustles over the bed sheets and my cheek slides along the pillowcase and my body opens like a flower before clenching down on him. The orgasm shoots through me with a vengeance.

My back bows before releasing like some crazy yoga move. My breath pours out of me, becoming a sob of release at the end, and with his bare hand he reaches under me, finds my clit and starts to rub – his touch much rougher than mine would be.

But his body slams into mine, all nuances lost – pure animal humping has commenced. He's lost his manners and his finesse and that is always what breaks me down to the sweetest spot, the place where I shiver at the power of my submission. The power I *have* over him.

'Come again,' he says, sounding like he's issuing some bizarre formal invitation. His rhythm is chaos, his breath a freight-train rumble. His fingers abuse my poor tender clit and I shut my eyes, feeling his urgency.

When a roar rips out of him and his body hunches tight to mine, I give him what he's demanded and he accents my pleasure by dragging one of his new toys along the meat of my ass. I feel the welt blossoming even as another spasm works through my cunt.

'Good girl,' he says, lips pressed to my ear.

He rolls to his side taking me with him. He curves his body to mine and I watch him peeling his lone glove off. It hits the floor with a muted clank. Somewhere in the bed is the one that had been splayed on my chest like a disembodied hand.

'You did well, Paula,' he says, his lips pressed to the back of my neck, making me shiver.

His fingers slide along the raised weal on my bottom and the pleasure that blooms from that tender skin is immense.

I turn to face him and snuggle close. He holds me always. Always after he puts me through a fear or a test or even just a good rough fuck. He always holds me and smoothes my hair and whatever skin he may have abused. There are kisses and chatter and words of love. All of it flows over me after the fact and when I look into his face – older but so much wiser than mine – I see adoration and understanding.

He wrings from me the things I'd normally rather die

than let out. Every cry, whimper and tantrum. Every fear, wish and hope. I tamp it down all day every day so the world only sees my calm and proper face. The fearless me. Until he peels back my layers and lays me bare ...

He's right. Lawrence is not a handsome man. He's a beautiful one.

When the Lights Go Out
Chrissie Bentley

I was expecting it this time, but I still caught my breath, suppressing the gasp that drove up from my gut and fighting, too, to control the instinctive jump as fingers stroked roughly up my thigh in the darkness. Three times, three tunnels, and each time we emerged back into the daylight, the tableau was the same; two strangers seated at opposite ends of the compartment, heads still bent over the books they'd brought to while away the journey. But when the lights went out, that was a different story.

I knew this route well, and I swear it has to be one of the most breathtakingly curious railroads imaginable. Picture seventy miles and two hours that wind through some of the loveliest mountain scenery in America, and then black half of it out with so many tunnels that it could almost pass for a subway system. Particularly on those occasions, like today, when nobody has bothered to replace the blown lightbulbs that would normally bring at least a modicum of lighting to the interior of the carriage.

So we plunged from dazzling day to stygian darkness, back and forth, bright and black, until the effect became borderline stroboscopic, and the rattle of the train became the soundtrack to some vast experimental art-rock conceit.

One that was growing increasingly tactile as the journey continued.

The first time it happened, I blamed my imagination for the whisper of pressure that traced the hem of my (admittedly very short) skirt, the ghost of a breeze or the gossamer touch of a curious insect. My hand reached down to brush the skin and I turned my head slightly to gaze out of the window in that way that people always do on trains, as they wait for the tunnel to end. I'd already forgotten the touch.

The second time, the sensation lingered longer, strayed a little higher, and there was a definite deliberation to it, as though a pair of fingers was dancing on the very edge of my thigh, and I was just too surprised to slap or say 'Hey'. So I waited in the darkness till we emerged back into sunlight and I glanced across at my travelling companion, the lone man who had boarded the same carriage as me. He did not move a muscle. My imagination again, then.

The third time there was no mistake. A soft scrape up my inner thigh, a pause and then an almost reluctant retreat as we approached the tunnel's end, and I say 'almost' because I found myself regretting it, even as I seethed with deep-seated outrage. How dare he do this, how dare he touch me, and, when the light returned to the carriage, my eyes were already fixed on the emergency brake handle that hung above the empty seat opposite. 'Once more,' my fury whispered within, 'do that once more and the whole train will find out.' But then I glanced over and he remained seated stock still, legs stretched out across the carriage floor, face tilted down towards his book, and, when I measured the distance between him and me, there was no way that anyone could move that fast.

But I was ready, I was waiting, and I was not going to say a word.

I said I know this route well, although it's a few years since I last rode it; since I uprooted myself from my end-of-the-line hometown community college to study art on the East Coast. And I knew it because, back then, this was the only reliable way out of town once the snows started in October, once the passes became impassable and even the gritters and snowploughs were tucked up until the thaw.

The railroad always ran, though, carving through the drifts with ploughs the size of houses, and only ever pausing while a work crew cleared the occasional avalanche. Once or twice a year, when the temperatures really dipped deep enough, you'd hear about an engine becoming becalmed because its fuel had literally frozen in the pipes, but another one would drag it out, emerging from the sidings that were carved out of the mountain's guts when this entire country was still wearing diapers. Normal service would be resumed before you knew it.

That was then. These days, the train runs for the benefit of tourists and enthusiasts alone, and never during the winter months. But the very prospect of a visit back to the town where I was born (elderly relatives, old friends, the usual) had filled me with nostalgias that I'd not expected to feel, and a trip on the train was the best way to start.

I wondered what my companion's reasons were. From his clothes I doubted he was a trainspotter, and from his apparent familiarity with the route itself, knowing when every tunnel was approaching, it was unlikely that he was a tourist, either. Although, who knows? He was probably wondering the same about me.

The tunnels vary in length. Some appear to stretch on for ever, although we'd not come to any of those yet. Others feel almost unnecessary, as if the original engineer simply couldn't resist boring his tracks through every rock that he came to, even though it would have been quicker and easier to dynamite them all out of sight.

Conservationists praise him now, pointing to the line as a supreme example of man working with nature, as opposed to simply blasting it into history. And I praised him too, because we'd flashed through three or four of those baby blacknesses now, and I didn't feel that touch. Another indication that my companion knew the line, another clue as to who he might be.

A railroad employee, maybe. Without appearing (I hoped) to be staring, I snuck another look over at him. I'd put him around my age, so sort-of-somewhere mid-thirties. His hair peeked dark from beneath his hat, and his boots were clean though they'd not been polished. He might be wearing a tie. Hard to tell; his chin kept his neckline in shadow. But he didn't appear too shabby, and he certainly didn't look the type whom you'd expect to find groping strange women on a Rocky Mountain train ride. Oh, and another thing. I'd swear he was sitting a bit nearer than the last time I looked, as though every time we went through a tunnel he'd inch himself just a little closer.

A knuckle grazed my panties, grazed my pussy through the cloth, and I fought back the yelp by biting down on my lip. Absorbed by my thoughts, I'd lost my bearings, and the next tunnel had crept up even more stealthily than he did. I cursed myself quietly; I'd resolved not to make a sound, and so far I'd more or less kept that up. But I'd also resolved not to move, yet my legs had still parted as his hand slipped between them – welcoming, maybe; curious, yes. I wanted to know how far this would go. I wanted to know how far *I* could go.

The knuckle lingered, light enough that I could almost shut my mind to its presence, firm enough that it would be able to feel the wetness and warmth that were embracing my pussy. I held my breath, not trusting myself to exhale as I waited to see what he would do next, and I was concentrating so hard on one thing that I didn't even notice something else. That his hand had moved away, he had moved away, and we were back into daylight with me sat there frozen, a tooth still pinning my bottom lip down and my legs still parted wide.

And he was maybe a little bit closer.

I wondered if I should speak. Nothing incriminating, nothing accusing, just a few friendly words to pass away the time. But I couldn't trust my voice to stay steady, and didn't believe I could keep my words light. Besides, I didn't want to break the spell, that heart-stopping moment when the hunter sights prey, because I hadn't yet decided who was who.

I looked out of the window at the landscape flashing by, placing it on the map that my memory sketched out. One of the big ones was coming up, one of the tunnels that drove straight through a peak, with a halt in the middle for the maintenance crews. A boyfriend and I once got off the train there, intending to explore the heart of the mountain. We wound up scaring ourselves silly with every ghost story that we'd ever heard, and didn't move from the platform until the next train arrived, eight long, cold and miserable hours later.

At least, that is what we told our parents when they asked us where we'd been all day, because neither of us dared to discuss what had really happened. How we'd found ourselves in a back room hewn from the living rock, with a light and a table and a couple of camp beds, a fridge with some beer, Cheese-Whiz and nachos, a Stephen King novel and some old dog-eared porn. It was where the maintenance guys went to relax between shifts, but there was no one around now and so what if there was? We weren't doing anything wrong.

I shifted in my seat, just enough to send a brief thrill of excitement bulleting into my abdomen, just enough to be ready for my companion's next assault.

That was the day I learned the strength there is in silence, in guiding my lover with inaction, not words, making him work for the pleasure of bringing me joy, while I thumbed through the porno and refused to bat an eyelid. Not even when I orgasmed.

And the point of that story is, now we'd see how good my companion really was. I knew about that little halt, so brightly lit up in the heart of the darkness. But did he?

We were rounding the curve now that led into the

tunnel and I braced myself. A knuckle last time; a finger this? I swallowed hard as my heart started to race, tensed as my pussy began pulsing expectantly, greasing the lips that would part in welcome.

I wanted him to touch me, to part me, to enter me. I wanted to feel his finger inside me while I sat immobile, frozen as my libido danced on the edge of triumph and lust, yet pinned into place by the sheer weight of his need. He wanted me and he was taking me, and, without a word, a gesture, or any sign that I even knew he existed, I was letting him.

Nothing.

I sat, he sat. I bit down on my lip again, shocking myself at the absurdity of my shock and, yes, disappointment, which fuelled a flash of anger that pierced even more sharply than the rage that had greeted his overtures.

Who does he think he is?

And then it was gone and I was blinking as the train slowed into the light of the halt, my nerve-ends relaxing as we stopped for a moment, and I allowed myself to breathe again as we lurched back into motion.

Breathe and relax.

He pinched. He pinched my clit. Through panties so moist they might as well have dissolved, thumb and forefinger were roughly gripping then twisting, and I buried my face in the arm that sprang instinctively out, holding it back with teeth in my wrist as I fought against the cry, fought against the struggle, forced myself to relax again. To ignore the pain that only hurt because there was no other word for the sensations that tore me. Uncomplaining and silent while he did what he wished, because that was what I wished as well. That was what I needed.

Daylight. I didn't require a mirror to tell me I was flushed, I could see my eyes wide in my reflection in the window. And him? Head still bowed, legs still stretched, he might have been sleeping, to anyone who glanced in to look at us. Sleeping while a mad woman sat wide-eyed and sweating maybe three feet away.

My mind flashed back to film class at school. An old, old short – an Edison, I think. A lady and her maid in a railway compartment, a gent sitting opposite, watching as they talked. Flashing through tunnels like we were. The difference was, every time they emerged back into the light, the tableau had shifted, the man growing bolder, the women growing wilder. And it ended with the gent in a clinch with the maid, while the lady simply went about her business.

Or is that what I wished had happened? Is that what I wanted to be happening now?

No. It was better this way. It was always better this way. A man will work harder to make you happy if you take his best shot and just wait for more. It makes him feel more like a man because you feel more like a lady, dignified and disdainful, daring him to do something and, this time, make it count. Come on, sonny, shatter my reserve.

So I would remain the lady, outwardly calm, aloof and unconcerned, keeping her feelings locked deep inside her because that was the encouragement her companion really sought, a sense of dominion, of power and strength, and not even a fleeting flicker of realisation that maybe he didn't have the control that he thought. That this was my game now, and my rules he was playing by. He would do the running, and he would run where I told him to.

Now he was inside me, his hand stretching my panty leg to the side and a finger as deep in my tunnel as the train was buried in its. Film class again; I'd always hated that analogy, wrote it off as lazy and corny, and I didn't like the space rockets or waterfalls either. Now the image haunted me, because what better one was there? Deliberate strength and irresistible motion. His finger felt endless as my pussy spread to welcome it, and, when a second one joined it, I did not even flinch.

Deep and deeper, my folds unfurling as my wet flesh sucked at the harsh intruder, and his finger was fucking me now, smooth rhythmic motions that filled me to bursting while my body begged silently for more.

His thumb was on my clitoris and every nerve in my body flocked to the spot, each jostling for the jolt of exquisite pressure that was pushing me towards the edge of paralysis. But only the edge. He knew what he was doing, teasing and tweezing, and convulsing me with shivers that I refused to acknowledge with even a gasp.

Would this tunnel never end?

He'd found a rhythm and it was driving me wild, a jackhammer pounding that didn't waver, just drove in and out, full steam ahead, and my flesh was ablaze and my nerve-ends were singing, a blur of movement that was blurring my senses, and an onrush of sensation that left me soaring and falling, and it doesn't matter how many times I've been fucked to a climax, getting there has never, ever felt like this.

My fists clenched, nails in my palms. How easy it would be to simply throw my body backwards, my legs parting wide, my hips bucking furiously, screaming for him to fuck me harder. But I stayed in my seat, stayed motionless and calm even as my body continued to tear itself apart from the inside.

Then it stopped. Then he stopped. We were out of the tunnel, he was back in his seat and, if his nostrils caught the scent of pussy that clung so thick to the air around us, they neither flared nor twitched in recognition.

I'll give him this. He's good.

But I'm better.

I needed to calm down. Trusting the noise of the train to drown the sound, I took a deep breath, holding the air in my lungs for the count of five, then gently exhaling. Again, but this time ten seconds. And again, until I was holding it for thirty and my heart rate had gone back to something like normal.

I shifted in the seat and felt it sodden beneath me. My book had slipped off my lap and lay on the seat beside me. I picked it up and leafed through, searching for my place. I had no intention of reading, and I couldn't if I'd tried. I wasn't even sure if I remembered where I'd got to in the story. For at least half of this journey, though my eyes had followed the words, I doubted I'd absorbed more than one in ten. But I had to do something to prove that I was still in control, and with my pussy screaming, cheated of the prize that had swum so agonisingly close, I stared down at the page.

Minutes passed. I glanced at my watch. Barring any delays between now and town, we would be there in about half an hour; thirty minutes which I measured in terms of a long uphill incline as we followed the river, and just two more tunnels, both of them long enough for … the thought trailed off, like an author overusing the ellipses.

Like I said before, blown bulbs weren't exactly unexpected on this line. In fact, it had once been something of a standing joke, even among the railroad staff. Growing up, I lost count of the number of make-out stories I heard from my friends, all of which happened on the train. Including a few of my own.

134

I smiled at memories that I'd not indulged for so long, remembered how every twist in the track flashed its own secret signal, a bit like the notebooks we girls would pass between us, detailing the exact cost in compliments, gifts, meals and movies of every conceivable thing a boyfriend might ask for. A burger at the diner earned one hand on your breast, and those buildings on the rocks over there; after ninety minutes of him kissing and pawing like an octopus, that was when you'd reward him with a hand that slipped downstairs.

Because, in the same amount of time it took to unbutton his Levis, the tunnel would swallow the train, and by the time it spit it out again – well, like I said, I hate railroad-as-a-metaphor-for-sex analogies, no matter how appropriate they may be. Then another ten minutes to tidy yourselves up, and you'd be stepping out on to the platform bright-eyed, bushy-tailed and very freshly fucked.

I wondered if my companion's friends had ever read the same notebook.

Resting my head on the rattling window, I could see the tunnel entrance approaching. In my mind, I began counting down the seconds, surprised how readily the old habit came back to me, and not at all surprised, as my mind framed 'zero', to feel rough hands grasping my wrists, pinning them against the coarse seat-back behind me. A mouth was on mine, hard and unyielding, forcing my lips to open around it as a lithe tongue slipped inside, liquid and serpentine, tasting of hunger and heat and tobacco.

I kissed back, my teeth grazing him, and my arms were wrenched upwards, held above my head as my wrists were transferred to the grip of one hand. The other stroked down my cheek, neck and breast, pinching nipples with a passion that I fought to ignore, but there was no hiding their hardness or their eager response.

His hand returned between my legs, pulling at my panties now and dragging them down. I raised my ass slightly, and felt the fabric slip away, binding my legs as it was pulled to my knees, before fingers fought roughly to reopen my thighs, spreading me wide as he grasped my wrists tighter. I gasped, but my sudden shock was devoured by his unending kiss, and his body moved closer, one foot forcing my panties to the ground and his legs parting mine as his fingers continued to thrust. The carriage had been dark before, now it was black as his body loomed over me, and I felt his presence overshadowing me, tall and greedy, brutal and hard.

He broke the kiss but his hand was still pounding, and then that stopped as well as he straightened himself, and I sensed his fingers moving to the buttons of his trousers, flicking them open as he reached in for his cock. I could feel its warmth as it sprang out from its cage, riding that sudden breath of musky sweat that sent a fresh spasm of want through my screaming wide cunt.

We hung there unmoving for moments like minutes. Occasionally, as the train jarred and jolted, there would be a tantalising touch of heat on my cheek, and my mind conjured images of that one eye staring wide, a trace of seeping pre-come stretched from my skin to his.

He was jerking himself slowly, deliberately, softly, hardening himself for whatever the next scene in the play was, and my arms were beginning to ache, still gripped in a fist that encircled both easily. I took a breath and inhaled his scent again, thick with desire and excitement and want. Masculinity. That's what romance writers mean when they use that word: the smell of a man, every one unique, but unmistakable too. The smell of the taste of the need of the hunger, and my mouth was watering as wet as my pussy, and still we were frozen – still life with desire – a moment that lasted for as long as a photograph, permanently fixed in the endless darkness.

My heart rose to my mouth, and my body took control, feeding from the images as they clattered through my mind. I felt myself soaring towards the precipice again. But was I really soaring? Or was I being borne, snatched up and carried there by the strength of his will, by his relentless drive, by his need to possess, by the ease with which his very presence grasped my emotions, my responses, my body?

Because that is what this was all about, a battle of wills, a trial of strength. In love as in life, and especially

137

in the darkness of a railroad tunnel with a stranger about
to fuck your throat, you are either going to take what
you want, or you will accept what you're given.

Right now, he thinks that he is on top.

Right now, he thinks he can take what he wants.

Right now, he thinks that he controls the night.

But I'm the one who grew up with these trains, and
I'm the one who remembers the day when they installed
the over-seat lighting. And if he raises my wrists just a
little bit more, as he will have to when he takes that
final step forward, as his cock comes in reach of my
greedy, grasping lips, my knuckles will be pressed against
the dollar-sized on-switch that is set into the wall.

And as I fold my mouth around his hardness, and he
startles blindly into bright, unexpected light, well, then
we will see who is left in the dark.

Dirty Pretty Underthings
Courtney James

Deric had been borrowing my panties again. Oh, he'd tried to disguise the fact, burying them halfway down the laundry basket, beneath his work shirts, where he thought I might not notice them. But as I emptied out the dirty clothes, ready to bundle them into the washing machine, his abuse of my underwear became all too apparent. The elastic waistband was stretched and baggy, and a thick, crusted white spot marred the soft sky-blue lace. I didn't need to sniff it to recognise it as come.

Once more, I found myself wondering why Deric felt the need to disguise his fetish from me. If he'd only broached the subject, I could have told him how exciting I found the thought of his hard cock poking out of soft, silky underwear, and how much more exciting it would

139

be – for both of us – if I were to force him into a pair of my panties. Deric was a submissive at heart, though he always fought shy of revealing his true inclinations. Or maybe – and my own black silk thong, so deliciously insubstantial where it clung to my pussy lips, grew damp as I pondered this – he wanted me to catch him in the act of parading around in my scanties and wring a confession of his needs from him. Well, if that was the game he wished to play, I'd more than happily take him on at it.

Like all good hunters in search of their prey, I set about baiting the trap I left for Deric with great care. While he toiled oblivious in his office, I spent an hour perusing the racks of lingerie in the grandest department store in town, searching for the perfect garment to catch his eye. Would he yearn to squeeze himself into the white nylon bikini-cut panties, so sheer as to be all but invisible, that would reveal every last contour of his cock and the bush of crisp dark hair surrounding it? What about the saucy high-legged, polka-dotted pair that would fit so snugly around his balls? Or maybe the knickers with the pale-pink ruffles, so feminine as to be almost ridiculous on a big, masculine frame like his? At last, I decided on the ruffles, though I tossed the other two pairs into my basket as a treat to myself, along with a half-cup bra, designed to proffer my small firm tits to my husband's greedy gaze, and a tight black waist-cincher I'd had my eye on for a while. Even with a sale reduction of 15 per cent, it was still so expensive the price tag made me take a sharp, shocked breath, but Deric's credit card could stand the cost.

Back home, I rang the firm we'd employed to install the new cupboards in our recently renovated kitchen, and asked them to send someone over to give me a quote for a walk-in closet in the master bedroom. It didn't surprise me to hear someone was available to measure up within the hour; I'd taken to wearing the shortest skirts I possessed when I'd made the workmen their morning brew, strutting around the kitchen with almost all of my long, shapely legs on display, and it had obviously made a memorable impression. Then I tossed the ruffled panties on the bed and went to make myself a cup of Earl Grey while I waited.

Deric always finishes at lunchtime on a Friday. Right on cue, I heard his BMW purr to a halt in the driveway, then, moments later, his key turning in the front door. Mentally, I followed his routine: briefcase stowed in the hall, shoes kicked off to lie beneath the coat rack, tie loosened as he climbed the stairs, mind on the shower he planned to take. I wished I could be in the bedroom to see his face as it registered the sight of the panties, left out so casually – or so it appeared. Would his cock be hardening in his charcoal suit trousers, his heart already pounding a little faster at the thought of touching those frivolous ruffles, of holding the garment to his nose to see whether it bore any of my feminine scent, of sliding the panties up his legs, learning for himself how soft and comfortable they were? How cruel of me, to place such temptation in his way, knowing he just wouldn't be able to resist.

When I walked into the bedroom, the scene that met my eyes was even more arousing than I'd imagined. Deric, his work clothes scattered on the floor around him, stood in front of the full-length mirror, admiring his panty-clad body from every angle. I'd never seen my husband preen before, but that's the only word that can adequately describe his behaviour at that moment. The underwear looked just as silly on him as I'd expected, but he really didn't care. His expression was dreamy, almost rapturous, as he ran a hand down over his flat, hairy belly, ready to slide it under the waistband of the panties and touch his erect cock where it lurked beneath the nylon ruffles.

'Deric, just what do you think you're doing?' I asked, adding just the right amount of feigned shock to my tone.

He started at the sound of my voice and turned to see me watching him from the doorway. The sweetest scarlet flush came to his face, and he hopped from foot to foot as he tried to stammer out some kind of explanation. But what could he say? I'd caught him wearing my panties, and if I hadn't been so sure he'd wanted this to happen, right from the very first time he'd filched one of my worn pairs of underwear from the laundry basket, I'd almost have felt sorry for him.

'So this is what you get up to when I'm not around?' As I walked into the bedroom, Deric was able to take a better look at the outfit I'd chosen to wear for this confrontation. A tight black dress that finished at mid-thigh was teamed with sheer black stockings and high patent heels, sophisticated and radiating cool self-control. Not the kind of clothes I usually favoured for a Friday afternoon spent pottering around the house, but this was no ordinary Friday.

'Zara, I don't know what to tell you,' he began.

'Well, don't tell me anything, then. Just shut up and listen while I give you my thoughts on what's been happening here, because this has been going on for far too long now. As I see it, you're just a dirty little panty fetishist. Sneaking round, trying on my undies when you think I'm not around, stretching them to the point where I'll never be able to wear them again … Do you know quite how foolish you look in those things?'

Deric stood, head bowed, meekly taking every lash of my waspish tongue as I detailed his flaws. He appeared to be relishing the verbal humiliation, if the way his cock fought to push its way over the waistband of the panties was an accurate guide. As for me, sticky heat suffused my pussy and my nipples were tight and crinkled, poking above the demi-cups of my new bra. I'd never dreamed Deric might derive such a strong thrill from being mocked and belittled, and I intended to put this information to very good use.

'Do you know what happens to sneaky little panty thieves like you, Deric?' I asked, moving close to him.

He shook his head, bare feet shuffling uneasily against the shagpile carpet. Not the response I required from him.

'I can't hear you, panty thief.'

'No, I don't know,' he murmured, still unable to meet my gaze.

'That's "I don't know, Mistress Zara" to you.' I don't know where the notion of styling myself his mistress had come from – sometimes these thoughts just pop into your head when circumstances are right – but it seemed wholly appropriate. Out in the working world, Deric was boss: he made the money, he made the decisions, he had dozens of people answering to him, and whatever instructions he gave were followed without question. Here in the bedroom, my word had become the only one that mattered, and for once, he would find himself doing as he was told.

'Sorry, Mistress Zara,' he stammered. 'It won't happen again, I promise.'

'And why should I believe your promises? There's only one way to ensure you learn that I simply won't tolerate this kind of behaviour, and that's to dish out the kind of punishment that will stop you doing it again.'

Was this the point where his fantasies parted company with the reality of being caught in my undies? Or did his cock give yet another excited surge as he considered all the possibilities of what might come next, from spanking to full-blown sissification? The latter I found a step too far – Deric might be a man in panties, but he was still all man, as far as I was concerned – but my gaze fell on the wooden-backed hairbrush lying on the dressing table, and my hands itched to snatch it up and bring it down hard on my husband's nylon-clad backside.

I would have done exactly that if I hadn't heard the doorbell ringing downstairs. I didn't immediately hurry to answer it; I knew who was calling, and I could afford to wait till they pressed the bell again, more insistently this time.

Deric didn't seem too concerned, no doubt assuming I was waiting for whoever was at the door to give up and go away. His face, which was in danger of settling into complacency, fell when I snapped, 'Aren't you going to get that?'

'But – but I can't. Not like this.' He shot a panicked glance down at his barely covered state.

'Oh, yes you can. You can – and you will. You'll go down and speak to whoever's standing there. And if you don't –' I brought out the cameraphone I'd been hiding behind my back and fired off a couple of quick snaps of Deric, standing helpless and humiliated in my panties '– well, I think the girls in your office might be very interested in seeing these, don't you?'

He looked at me in mute, supplicating appeal, but my expression gave no indication as to whether I would carry out my threat. Deciding not to risk it, he all but scampered down the stairs. I followed at a more leisurely pace and leaned over the balcony on the landing to watch him open the door with fumbling fingers. He did his best to disguise his body from passers-by, shielding himself with the front door, and I mentally added another stroke to his punishment for such coyness.

I couldn't see Deric's face, but the expression on that of the man who followed him inside was all too clear. Shock quickly gave way to something between amusement and contempt as he registered just what my husband had on.

'All right, Mr Parkinson?' Warren from the building firm sauntered into the hall, walking with the brash swagger I remembered from his time working on our kitchen. They couldn't have known it, but they'd sent the perfect man for the scenario I had in mind. Warren was confident to the point of arrogance, and prided himself on being a ladies' man. His conversation, at least when I'd been in earshot, had barely risen above crotch level, but I wasn't looking for a master of witty repartee to assist me this afternoon. I wanted someone who let his dick make all the decisions, and Warren fitted the stereotype perfectly. 'Your missus rang, said she wanted a quote, but I can see I've caught you in the middle of something, so perhaps I ought to –'

'No, no, that's fine, Warren,' I said, making stately progress halfway down the stairs. 'We're all ready for you. Do show Warren upstairs, won't you, Deric?'

Out of Warren's eyeline, I waved my phone in Deric's direction, reminding him of the incriminating evidence it contained. With what sounded like a definite whimper, Deric turned and led our guest up to the bedroom.

'So, is it just a single closet you're wanting?' Warren asked as he surveyed the room, clearly still believing he was here on a job. 'Because I could do you a lovely set of fitted cupboards along that whole back wall ...' He whipped out his tape measure, at which point I stopped him.

'Thank you, Warren, but all I really want you to do is sit on the bed and watch for a while.' I patted the coverlet, and he did as I asked.

He sat with legs splayed wide, drawing my attention to the prominent package at his crotch, wrapped in faded denim. He might have been rough and ready, dark hair too thickly gelled for my liking and a cheap-looking gold ring glittering in his left earlobe, but the sheer bulk of him was enticing, as was the scent that lingered on his skin, fresh wood shavings and good, honest sweat. He'd be the type to throw you down on the bed, holding his hard cock like a weapon, primed and ready to stab you to the core, as he told you to spread them, sweetheart ...

'You see,' I continued, dragging my mind back to the matter in hand with some effort, 'I caught my miserable creep of a husband trying on my panties, and it's not the first time he's done it, not by any means. The best part is he thinks he looks good in them.' I gave a contemptuous snort. 'What do you think, Warren? Look at those ridiculous hairy legs of his, and the bulge his puny cock is making in the front.'

Deric's face, already beet-red, turned another shade darker at the sound of the builder's mocking laugh. If I'd feared making a misstep by bringing a third party into this scene, compounding my husband's frustration even further, the reaction of both men had vindicated the decision. Deric was so tightly wound by each fresh torment, I suspected I only had to press my fingers to his crotch and he'd be coming in his frilly panties, while Warren had settled back to enjoy the show. From the looks he kept sneaking at my stocking-clad legs, I had the feeling he wanted to enjoy something more intimate, too, if only I'd give him the green light. All in good time, I thought.

'So, Deric, what were we discussing before Warren joined us?'

He fidgeted, plucking at the ruffles on his panties in his agitation. 'Um – er – you were telling me I deserved to be punished,' he replied in a voice barely above a whisper.

'Speak up,' I urged him. 'Warren can't hear you. And didn't you forget something when you addressed me?'

'Yes, I'm sorry. I – I deserve to be punished, Mistress Zara.' This time my husband's tone was loud and clear.

'Indeed you do. More than that, you deserve to be punished in front of an audience.'

Glancing over at Warren, I saw him biting back a chuckle as the implications sunk in. He'd just realised he was about to see my husband get his arse whacked, and the prospect clearly amused him.

'Bend over, Deric,' I ordered.

He didn't disobey, but quickly assumed a hands-on-knees position that presented his backside beautifully. I took my implement of choice, the hairbrush, from the dressing table, and slapped it against my palm a couple of times. Deric didn't look up at the sound, just whimpered again, resigned to his fate.

'This is for wearing my panties without my permission.' I swatted both his cheeks in quick succession, the brush's broad, flat back spreading the sting over a considerable area of flesh, judging by Deric's pained, yelping reaction. 'And this is for not having the common courtesy to admit to me you're nothing more than a wretched, knicker-sniffing worm.' A more prolonged volley of blows followed my pronouncement, causing Deric to hop in place, wanting to rise from his bent-over position but not daring to risk my further wrath. As if he had any hope of avoiding that.

When I paused for breath, he must have thought his spanking was over and was no doubt priding himself on how well he'd taken it. I quickly disabused him of the notion by yanking down his panties and baring his bottom, now mottled red and hot to the touch. He almost sobbed aloud at this fresh humiliation. Warren leaned forward, keen to get a better look at the marks I'd left on my husband's arse.

'And these –' I raised my arm for a final time before launching into a renewed assault on his buttocks '– are for never confessing that you want to watch me being fucked by another man.'

If he'd said anything to indicate that wasn't one of his cherished fantasies, I would have called a halt to the game, thanked Warren for his time and sent him away. But when Deric looked up at me, there might have been tears shining in his eyes, but there was also a weird little smirk on his lips that let me know I'd drilled down deep and found the mother lode.

'Go and stand in the corner,' I ordered him. 'Put your hands on your head, don't look in my direction and don't you dare pull your panties up.'

He shuffled over to the corner without a word. He must have known how foolish he looked, with the panties down round his knees and his freshly punished arse on display, but I'd seen the strength of his erection and knew he was loving every minute of his debasement.

'So, Warren,' I purred, turning my attention to our visitor, 'what does a woman have to do to get a decent fuck around here?'

The answer, it seemed, was to let him pull me into a tight, groping embrace. As he did, I could feel his erection, thick and solid where it lurked in his jeans. He made short work of stripping my dress from me, before pushing me to the bed and peeling down my panties. He left my bra on, telling me he liked the way my breasts jiggled on top of the cups, like two scoops of dairy vanilla.

His own clothes were discarded without ceremony, revealing an admirably hard body, honed by manual work. Not that Deric was running to fat, by any means, but he didn't have the delightful planes and ridges of muscle my fingers encountered as they explored Warren's broad chest and back.

Kneeling over me, he grabbed his cock and gave me the chance to worship it with my eyes, just as I'd foreseen. He had the inches, all right; he just had to know what to do with them. I'd demanded a decent fuck, after all. The last thing I required was a whip-it-in, whip-it-out merchant.

Though Warren didn't have as much finesse as I'd have liked, shoving home with a fierce thrust that made me squeal, his roughness was just what I needed at that moment. So wet my juices had dribbled down my thighs, I bounced and writhed on the bed, his thick shaft stretching me enough to give me all the friction I craved.

From time to time, he broke off from fucking me to aim a shout over at Deric. 'Hey, mate, your wife's got a gorgeous tight cunt. Bet you wish it was your cock all the way up it, rather than mine, eh?' If Warren was turning a husband into a cuckold for the very first time, he was a natural at it.

Deric didn't say anything but, when Warren resumed his frantic thrusting, I saw him look over at us, his expression a perfect mixture of lust, envy and adoration.

Warren flipped me over, getting me on all fours. His cockhead bumped against the entrance to my arse, sending a thrill of alarm and anticipation through me. 'What do you reckon, mate?' he asked Deric. 'Should I do your wife in the tradesman's entrance?'

For one delicious moment, I thought he actually might, then he slipped his cock back into my pussy. I knew he couldn't be far from his peak; running a hand down to the point where our bodies joined, I felt the tightness in his balls, sensed the effort he was making to hold back just a little longer. Still he fought to keep his strokes hard

152

and even, pounding me with just the right measure of intent. My fingers strayed to my clit, the bud tight and receptive. A swift rubbing motion, back and forth, round and around, was all it took to have the muscles in my pussy clenching round Warren's shaft, my heart beating a triumphant tattoo as the hot waves of bliss carried me away. Dimly, I heard Warren roar out his own climax, panting and cursing as he shot his come deep inside me, but I was too lost in my own pleasure to really care.

Deric didn't come at that point, even though I might have expected him to, driven to distraction by the sight of another man planting his seed in me. No, he came when Warren had left and I lay on the bed, still wearing my bra and stockings, Deric's head buried in my pussy as he licked all the spunk from my well-used hole. Tugging at his cock, he spurted his own tribute to my wicked imagination and dominant streak all over the coverlet. Of course, I made him lick that up, too, in between fervent promises to keep his filthy hands out of my lingerie drawer in future.

So it was decided. Deric wouldn't be borrowing my panties again. From now on, he'd have his own personal collection of pretty underthings, perfect for wearing under those sober business suits of his. I didn't know quite yet what that collection would contain, though I had plenty of ideas. Ideas about French knickers and low-rise shorts and the skimpiest of knickers. And if I had my way

– and, even as I thought that, I realised *if* was no longer in question – Deric would find himself discussing every one of them with one of the pretty little assistants in the lingerie department where I'd been shopping this morning, before heading into the changing room for a private fitting. Smiling at the prospect of all the delicious public humiliation my panty-wearing husband had in store, I went to run myself a nice scented bath.

Fuck Around the Clock
Heather Towne

It was your typical sunny, leafy, suburban, Mid-American neighbourhood. The houses were new, built just after the war, the lawns green and lush and neatly trimmed like the hedges, a gentle breeze rustling the trees, birds singing pleasant tunes from the branches. If atomic annihilation hung over the nation, they hadn't heard about it here, or they didn't care. Ike was ensconced in the Oval Office and the living was easy, the warm, contented stupor palpable.

Only, behind the *Good Housekeeping* facades, the aluminium siding and plate-glass windows and fake-oak doors, other things besides dusting and napping and TV viewing were going on, other things besides prayers being said; darker, deeper things; way, way kinkier things.

Like the old lady with all the cats in 609. She was petting her pussy, all right – her own pussy. The curlers were out and the housecoat off, the dyed-red dame holed up in her bathroom clasping a tit in one hand and rubbing her twat with the other, making herself purr with pure sexual feeling.

For a woman of sixty, she wasn't bad-looking: slender body, firm, fairly smooth skin, handsome face; and very active. Her breasts drooped, but that just made them easier to push up, plant a hard red nipple in her kisser and suck on it. She sank three long, slim digits right inside her slit and sawed away. The toilet and the bathroom walls rocked with her self-induced orgasm, making the cats yowl and scratch at the door in alarm.

Two houses down and two generations removed, a pair of corn-fed college students were supposed to be studying, or maybe drooling over that dreamboat math professor of theirs, or gazing longingly at the poster of the 'Wild One', Marlon Brando, hanging up on the wall over the bed. A towering elm provided visual access to the blonde girl's upstairs window, and it was easy to see that the curious co-eds were more interested in doing each other than their calculus homework. They sat on the edge of the bed with their arms entwined around one another, their tongues earnestly kissing and frenching and fondling. Just two hot-blooded teenaged girls exploring their Sapphic passion while they had the house all to themselves.

156

The blonde was tall and thin and tanned, built along Varsity athletic lines, her pale brunette companion smaller, curvier, more bookwormish with her glasses and chubby cheeks. They excitedly pulled the ribbons out of their hair and plied sweaty hands up their school sweaters. Then the sweaters, poodle skirts, penny loafers and bobby-sox were sent flying, along with their modest cotton underpinnings, as the two girls got really industrious.

Blondie eagerly sucked on the brunette girl's tits, working the thick young flesh with her hot brown hands, pulling on the flushed, cherry-red nipples with her pouty lips. Then Raven pushed the other girl down on to her bed, and they rolled around tight together, totally naked, sucking slippery pink tongues and squeezing ripe dimpled bum cheeks, rubbing fuzzy wet muffs.

They did the math, and it all added up to absolute lesbianism: sweet sixty-nine. The girls got oral where it really counted, the blonde on top and the brunette down below, heads between legs and tongues licking twats. The bed trembled like their sweet bodies, as they lapped and sucked each other to squirting, neato-keen orgasm.

The scene down in the rec room of 632 was even rawer, raunchier, nothing innocent about it at all. Four consenting adults who knew exactly what they were doing: four men. Two were down on the beige shag carpet, on all fours, facing each other and swapping spit, while the other two crouched behind them, having just a gay old time nailing the kneeling men's asses. Cocks pounded into bums, splitting and rippling firm apple cheeks, deep-drilling hot sucking chutes.

The two 'roommates' who shared the house had been so excited to receive their new playmates that they hadn't taken the time to fully curtain off one of the basement windows. There was a gap, large enough to exploit.

The men traded places, bottoms becoming tops, the other pair of bottoms getting stuffed, and chuffed. Sweat glistened on the crouching men's lean, taut bodies, shafts shining as they urgently pumped in and out. The two men now getting reamed, for perhaps the first time, resided in 703 and 705 respectively, with their nuclear families.

Good neighbours sharing good times, exploring new frontiers. Happy days for one and all.

The pool table became a fuck table, four balls banging into the rear pockets. The married family men sprawled on their backs, kissing one another again, their hairy chests heaving, heavy cocks jumping, as the two seasoned, shaven guys shouldered legs and shunted their cocks back and forth in violated manholes.

The fucked men gripped each other's pricks, frantically pumped in rhythm to the anal pumping they were receiving. Then they grunted, hollered, thick ropes of semen exploding out of their hand-cranked dongs, the other two men hammering their ecstatic points home.

The fuckers shook and shouted themselves, blowing out their balls, coating bowels.

Just your typical sleepy, sleazy, All-American, suburban neighbourhood.

My scouting expeditions had yielded those scorching scenarios, but my real focal point was number 624, the home of Mrs Margaret Cooney, the woman I'd been hired to watch. Hubby Herbert thought maybe the missus was cheating on him, leaving the home looking for love, while he was slaving away at the insurance mines. My speciality is surveillance, the man's money my ticket to eyeball.

Only, while I'd spied with my little eye that the rest of the neighbourhood was a seething sexpit beneath the deceptively serene surface, I'd observed that the goings-on in 624 were strictly sedate. Margaret didn't seem to do anything – except her nails, her hair and her legs. She spent most of Day One sitting on the couch watching television or reading a magazine or catching up on more beauty sleep. She didn't even make poor Herbert breakfast, clean up the dishes, dust or vacuum, from what I could see. And I could see it all, through the picture window in front and the kitchen window in back.

Day Two, a furniture truck rolled up into the driveway.

Herbert had told me they were expecting a delivery: a brand-new leather recliner for hard-working Margaret. From the vantage point of my white-panelled, dark-windowed van just up the street, I watched two men climb out of the cab of the olive-green one-ton. It was another clear, bright day in suburbia, perfect for ogling the pair of beefy furniture movers as they dismounted and strode around to the rear of the truck.

They were both tall and well built, wearing identical white T-shirts with logos and denim pants, their muscular arms sunkissed nut-brown like their rugged faces. I honed right in on them with the telescopic lens attached to my Leica. One hunk had short, lustrous black hair, wide-set grey eyes, a Roman nose and a granite chin. The other heaping helping of man was blond, buzzcut, with high cheekbones and a cleft chin, sea-green eyes that exuded tropical heat.

My palms grew moist, nipples hard. The studs swung the back doors of the truck open, climbed inside and wrestled the recliner to the edge of the cargo bay. Then they jumped down, lifted the chair up and out and carried it to the front door of the red, white and blue home slumbering in the sun.

I took plenty of snapshots, for my own benefit. The way those mass-mounded butt cheeks bulged out those tight jeans, clenching and clutching; the sinewy bare arms and clothed broad backs bunching and flexing; the grimaces of sweaty exertion on the men's handsome faces – it was a sight to behold, and to capture for future appreciation.

But it was all strictly business for the beautiful boys in the sexy workduds, routine neighbourhood activity.

Until Mrs Margaret Cooney answered the bell and appeared at the front door, dressed in a black leather bustier and black leather panties and black leather boots, a studded choker around her neck, motorcycle cap atop her head, cat o' nine tails in her hand. And a smirk of evil delight on her gleaming red lips.

I almost cracked the camera lens against the tinted window, my pupils widening to full exposure, breath catching in my lungs. It was as unexpected as a tarantula on a slice of angel food cake.

The woman's breasts stretched out the shiny, laced bodice, all of her creamy-white cleavage and most of her dairy-sized tits on display. The panties were so brief and tight I could see the outline of her pussy lips beneath the glossy black surface, her fleshy thighs flared out for all to see. The boots were laced up to her knees, as highly polished and highly charged as the rest of her provocative get-up, and the motorcycle cap tilted jauntily to the right on her billowing black hair. She smacked the frayed ends of the leather whip against her open left palm, canting her hips and licking her lips, eyeing the men and the chair with equal and open lust.

The guys strained, sweated, holding up the heavy brown chair, waiting for a signal from the woman. They didn't seem the least bit surprised to see her dolled up in that dominating fashion, just expectant.

Margaret sneered and climbed aboard the chair. The

men carried her aloft inside the house and kicked the door shut behind them.

I was so stunned I just sat there gasping for air for a full minute, camera and face pressed up against the fogged glass, hardly believing what I'd just witnessed. I came to my senses quickly, though, eager to witness more. My client demanded it, after all.

I burst out of the back of the van and streaked across the street and up the driveway, using the big furniture truck as cover. I flung myself against the front of the house, alongside the picture window. I let the hot rush of tingling blood suffuse my pussy and swell my lips, then spun round and poked my head and camera around the window frame.

The men were parading Margaret all around the spacious living room, up on her chair, like she was the Sultana of Brunei or something. She was looking for just the perfect spot to set the new piece of furniture. But she, and I, could hardly take our eyes off the men – who were now totally and blazingly naked.

Their bodies looked even better without the restrictive work clothes, buff and brown and rippling, breathtakingly rounded and deep-split in back, heart-stoppingly long and jutting out front. The guys' cocks stood out from their hairy loins in full and utter erection, bobbing and wagging delectably as they wandered about the living room with the chair at the whim of the woman enthroned.

I took pictures with my glassy eyes, then my jumping camera. And the picture got still better, hotter, when Margaret at last located the exact right place for the recliner and had the boys set it, and her, down. Because then, after they'd helped her up to her feet, she snapped red metal cock rings around their mighty hard-ons, latched steel chains on to the rings and strung them out ten feet or so. She proceeded to pull the men around by the chains, by their cocks, getting them to rearrange all of her furniture.

It was every woman's fantasy: ordering gorgeous nude men around so that they set up an entirely new living-room ensemble for her.

Margaret jerked on the men's cocks from the comfort of her brand-new chair, smacking their bare bums with the whip when they ventured too close at her command, eyeing the sweaty muscular spectacle of all that heaving and pushing and lifting and shifting. It was like a work-men's ballet, with dominatrix Margaret lead choreographer and puppet-mistress.

Finally, the surly suburban housewife had her living room just as she wanted it (for the time being). And she proceeded to reward her humble servants – by savagely slashing and spanking them.

I cringed, crouching beneath the windowsill, capturing it all on camera and eyeball lenses. Watching as Margaret stood the two tall men in front of her – their cocks jutting out at her – and blistered their popping pecs with her cat o' nine tails.

She lashed one muscle-striated chest, then the other, the leather straps of her whip smacking against the hard, humped flesh with a practised, perverted flick of her wrist. The men stood hard and unflinching, taking it with barely a grimace of pain, or pleasure. I could clearly see their nipples puffing higher, however, the white streaks as the tendrils slashed across their tanned flesh, then the burning red marks that flamed up afterwards as Margaret branded them.

It was an eye-popping and cunt-wetting spectacle, available to anyone with the audacity to look through the surface of the crystal-clear picture window on the snug little bungalow at the dangerously dirty goings-on taking place within. I lapped it up like a tabloid photographer.

Margaret directed her aim lower. She flogged her way down the men's stolid bodies, whipping ribbed abs and flattened lower stomachs, lashing mucho-manly cocks. My breath caught in my heaving lungs, the camera jumping like it was taking earthquake footage, as Margaret began her leather assault on the pair of hunks' cocks.

She flayed their straining erections, moving alongside their chiselled nakedness and flipping the whip-ends over their dicks. The leather fingers wrapped around vein-ribboned shafts, seized tight, pulled, then slipped off, leaving twitching, towering, heated cocks behind. One at a time, over and over.

The woman was a virtuoso at the song of the whip, playing a wickedly erotic tune on the men's meaty instruments with every furious flick. Until she was flinging pre-come out of the gaping slits on the mushroomed cockheads with every flash of her wrist.

That's when she went easier, or harder, on the men. The mad housewife suddenly gently stroked their raging cocks with the frayed ends of her whip, top and bottom, polishing their shafts even harder and shinier. She tickled their balls to tightened intensity as well.

'Turn around!' she barked, making the men jump – to obey her command.

They spun around, showing their cheeky backsides to their hard-driving mistress. Those heavily mounded, heapingly built backsides that quivered with tautness and lushness, big and bold as brass. Margaret stood alongside the paired pair and flailed one set of cheeks with her whip, then the other splendid set.

I bit my lip, blinking in rhythm to the rise and fall of the lash, my camera shooting all on its own. Margaret was just as skilled at fanning and flaming butt-flesh as she was at cock and pec-meat. The men's sculpted bodies quivered slightly now at each scorching slash, getting burned in back like they had on the flip, fucking, side.

Margaret's wide eyes gleamed with the mania of the matronly dominatrix plying her trade at fever pitch. Her breasts shuddered with every heavy blow she landed down and across beautiful buttocks, her white teeth set and showing, nostrils flared to suck oxygen, legs trembling. I could almost hear the heavy breathing, hers and that of her pained and pleasured playmates, above my own, could clearly hear the strike of her whip, just about feel the stinging explosion of joy vibrating through the wall and the window.

Margaret yelled at the men. They bent forward, planting their hands on their thighs, pushing their beaten bums out for further punishment. She beat them still more, and more, leather whipping ferociously across electrified butt skin.

Then, abruptly, it ended. Margaret lowered her flailing arm, let the whip hang hot and empty.

She reached out with her left hand and touched the blond's bottom. He jumped, self-consciously, his buttocks tremoring deliciously, the transition from brutal to gentle too much to hide. Margaret caressed the marked agony and eroticism she'd flayed on to the man's glutes, a sneer on her glossy lips. She touched and rubbed the brunette's blazing butt, obviously enjoying the feel of the ridged results of her discipline.

She stuck the whip handle in between the men's legs and scrubbed their balls and cracks. Their cocks surged up into the air on the other side, pumped and primed beyond belief, for Margaret to put to better use than just pummelling.

I was so engrossed in the action myself, capturing it all on film and in memory, that I hardly heard the car pull up on the street, a door slam. Only the brisk, businesslike clicking of Oxfords on cement driveway, on the other side of the truck, alerted me at the last second to the fact that someone else was approaching the house: hubby Herbert.

I dropped down behind the rose bushes just in the nick of time. Mr Cooney walked right past me and up the flagstone path that led to the front door of his home dirty home. He opened the door and went inside.

I gritted my teeth, perspiration prickling my pensive face, gripping my camera like it'd offer me any protection from the explosion to come inside. I only prayed that, as a guilty bystander, I wouldn't suffer too much collateral damage.

I heard yelling – Margaret – the angry crack of flesh slapping flesh.

No gunshots, no body flying through the front window.

I ventured up off my knees and put face back to pane.

Things had gone from wicked to wild.

Herbert stood in a corner of the room, his balding head bowed, teary blue eyes rolled up to look at his wife and her two male slaves. She was standing tall in the centre of her remodelled living room, legs apart and fists on her hips, looking at her cowering husband with obvious contempt. Her leather panties were strewn on the hardwood floor. The blond hunk was behind her, on his knees, the brunette kneeling in front of her – one man eating out Margaret's pussy, the other her ass.

My eyes bugged and my nipples popped, pussy surging with shimmering glee. The blond had Margaret's plush butt cheeks spread wide with his hands and was using his wide tongue to paintbrush her bum cleavage, power-licking the woman's intimate, sensitive stretch of crack skin. Meanwhile, the brunette had flowered Margaret's pussy to full pink blossom with his strong fingers, and was lapping at the woman's *most* intimate, sensitive strip of skin.

Margaret stood there and took the lusty tongue-lashing with hardly a tremble, gasp or ripple, glaring at her cuckolded husband.

Well, I wasn't about to just crouch there and take it, without fully appreciating the sizzling tableau. So, while I held the camera up in my left hand, I plunged my right hand inside my shorts and my panties, striking hot, wet, wanton pussy. I shuddered, shuttered; snapping pics and scrubbing clit. Hands-on investigative work.

Margaret yelled something at Herbert. He stumbled humbly forward, unfastened his grey flannel suit pants and let them sag. His cock sprung out and up like an obscene pink exclamation point on the whole surreal, sensual proceedings.

The guy wasn't a bad-looking stiff, above or below the beltline. Round pale face and full red lips and cute button nose, a short, stocky body, smooth, thick shaft and bulbous, bloated crown.

Margaret whipped his dick, lacing the leather tendrils around his shaft like long black fingers, then unravelling them again with whiplash action, as she wrenched her hand back. She flogged her husband's straining erection, making the guy groan and buckle, beg for more. The one kneeling man lapping her snatch, the other kneeling man licking her crack.

My buffing hand bulged out my shorts, my swelled-up nipples testing the material strength of my top. The camera clicked away at lightning speed, my eye glued to the viewfinder for total exposure.

The scene went incendiary.

Margaret snarled something at her two slaves, and they stood up, licking their lips. She dragged them by the cocks over to the new recliner hubby had paid for, got the blond to recline full length on top of the expensive piece of furniture. She yanked his dick up by wrapping the chain around her fist. And then she got the brunette to help her on to that prong, backwards, the oiled tool pushing, popping inside her butt. She lay back on the laid-out man, his cock sinking inside her ass, her butt cheeks splaying out on his waist. The other man quickly moved in between their legs at her order, filling Margaret's pussy with his hardened tool.

I gulped, hooked two fingers inside my own sopping sexbox, right down to the knuckles. It was nothing compared to what Mad Margaret was getting stuffed with, but it did the trick just fine. Heat shimmered through my quivering body in waves, pumped out from my churning fingers up my cooch.

The men fucked Margaret front and back, the woman whipping them on, balling their chains in her fist. The brunette gripped her thighs and pounded his cock into her pussy, the blond thrusting his hips at the same fearsome pace, pistoning Margaret's anus. She screamed at her husband, and Herbert hustled closer, alongside. She snapped the leather fingers around his prick again, and he danced, ejaculating, spraying out his cuckolded lust all over his wife's double-penetrated, leather-clad body.

Margaret sneered, snorted, snarled, ass getting slammed and pussy rammed, breasts shuddering. She jerked on the chains attached to the cocks pumping her, and the two men spasmed, their muscles straining to the snapping points as they blasted out their own submissive joy into Margaret's butt and cunt.

She took it all without breaking sadistic character, getting creamed and craving more. But it was all too much for this clean-cut girl. I touched thumb to puffy pink trigger and went off like the Fourth of July.

I was rocked back on my heels, shockwaves of orgasm searing me, camera jumping right out of my hand. I gaped with naked eye at the three men showering, shooting their mistress full of sticky worship. And then cleaning up after themselves!

* * *

Herbert admitted he'd hired me just to watch. Almost as much as being cuckolded by his slave-driving wife, the guy got off on knowing that someone was watching him get humiliated while his spouse got fucked.

And to think he looked like such a respectable, upstanding member of the community. On the outside.

I gave him all of the hundreds of pictures I'd taken, saving the negatives for myself, of course. Because what I didn't tell the dear, dirty little man was that I'm not really a licensed investigator of any kind. I'm just an expert at surveillance thanks to a raging voyeurism fetish. If I can make a few extra bucks from my peccadillo – watching cheating husbands and wives and their naughty neighbours in action – so much the better.

Much like that peaceful, picture-perfect, suburban neighbourhood of Herbert's, beneath this girl's wholesome Nancy Olson exterior lurks the throbbing, twisted, towering passion of a pervert.

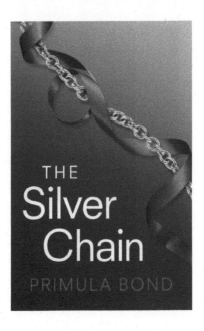

THE SILVER CHAIN – PRIMULA BOND

Good things come to those who wait…

After a chance meeting one evening, mysterious entrepreneur Gustav Levi and photographer Serena Folkes agree to a very special contract.

Gustav will launch Serena's photographic career at his gallery, but only if Serena agrees to become his companion.

To mark their agreement, Gustav gives Serena a bracelet and silver chain which binds them physically and symbolically. A sign that Serena is under Gustav's power.

As their passionate relationship intensifies, the silver chain pulls them closer together. But will Gustav's past tear them apart?

A passionate, unforgettable erotic romance for fans of *50 Shades of Grey* and Sylvia Day's *Crossfire Trilogy*.

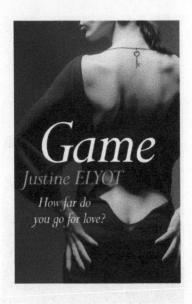

GAME – JUSTINE ELYOT

The stakes are high, the game is on.

In this sequel to Justine Elyot's bestselling *On Demand*, Sophie discovers a whole ne
world of daring sexual exploits.

Sophie's sexual tastes have always been a bit on the wild side – something her
boyfriend Lloyd has always loved about her.

But Sophie gives Lloyd every part of her body except her heart. To win all of her,
Lloyd challenges Sophie to live out her secret fantasies.

As the game intensifies, she experiments with all kinds of kinks and fetishes in a bid
understand what she really wants. But Lloyd feature in her final decision? Or will th
ultimate risk he takes drive her away from him?

Find out more at www.mischiefbooks.com

POWER PLAY – CHARLOTTE STEIN

ow she's the boss, everything that once seemed forbidden is possible…

Meet Eleanor Harding, a woman who loves to be in control and who puts Anastasia Steele in the shade.

en Eleanor is promoted, she loses two very important things: the heated relationship she had with her boss, and control over her own desires.

e finds herself suddenly craving something very different – and office junior, Ben, ems like just the sort of man to fulfil her needs. He's willing to show her all of the things she's been missing – namely, what it's like to be the one in charge.

Now all Eleanor has to do is decide…is Ben calling the kinky shots, or is she?

Find out more at www.mischiefbooks.com

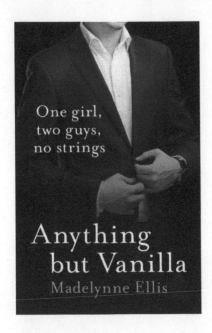

One girl,
two guys,
no strings

Anything
but Vanilla

Madelynne Ellis

ANYTHING BUT VANILLA
MADELYNNE ELLIS

One girl, two guys, no strings.

Kara North is on the run. Fleeing from her controlling fiancé and a wedding she n~~ever~~
wanted, she accepts the chance offer of refuge on Liddell Island, where she soo~~n~~
catches the eye of the island's owner, erotic photographer Ric Liddell.

But pleasure comes in more than one flavour when Zachary Blackwater, the char~~ming~~
ice-cream vendor also takes an interest, and wants more than just a tumble in the s~~and.~~

When Kara learns that the two men have been unlikely lovers for years, she beco~~mes~~
obsessed with the idea of a threesome.

Soon Kara is wondering how she ever considered committing herself to just one m~~an.~~

Find out more at www.mischiefbooks.com